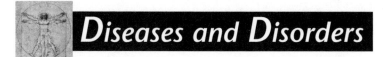
Diseases and Disorders

Breast Cancer

Titles in the Diseases and Disorders series include:

Diseases and Disorders

Breast Cancer

by Don Nardo

I respectfully dedicate this book to my wife and best friend, Christine, a woman of uncommon wisdom, sensitivity, and compassion, whose research help and constant advice during its writing were invaluable.

Library of Congress Cataloging-in-Publication Data

Nardo, Don.
    Breast cancer / by Don Nardo.
        p. cm. — (Diseases and disorders series)
Includes bibliographical references and index.
Summary: Discusses the risk factors, diagnosis, treatment, and survival rates of breast cancer, as well as research on the disease.
    ISBN 1-56006-905-8
    1. Breast—Cancer—Juvenile literature. [1 Breast—Cancer.
2. Cancer. 3. Diseases.] I. Title. II. Series.
    RC280.B6 N36   2002
    616.99'449—dc21

2001003672

Table of Contents

"The Most Difficult Puzzles Ever Devised"

CHARLES BEST, ONE of the pioneers in the search for a cure for diabetes, once explained what it is about medical research that intrigued him so. "It's not just the gratification of knowing one is helping people," he confided, "although that probably is a more heroic and selfless motivation. Those feelings may enter in, but truly, what I find best is the feeling of going toe to toe with nature, of trying to solve the most difficult puzzles ever devised. The answers are there somewhere, those keys that will solve the puzzle and make the patient well. But how will those keys be found?"

Since the dawn of civilization, nothing has so puzzled people—and often frightened them, as well—as the onset of illness in a body or mind that had seemed healthy before. A seizure, the inability of a heart to pump, the sudden deterioration of muscle tone in a small child—being unable to reverse such conditions or even to understand why they occur was unspeakably frustrating to healers. Even before there were names for such conditions, even before they were understood at all, each was a reminder of how complex the human body was, and how vulnerable.

While our grappling with understanding diseases has been frustrating at times, it has also provided some of humankind's most heroic accomplishments. Alexander Fleming's accidental discovery in 1928 of a mold that could be turned into penicillin has resulted in the saving of untold millions of lives. The isolation of the enzyme insulin has reversed what was once a death sentence for anyone with diabetes. There have been great strides in combating conditions for which there is not yet a cure, too. Medicines can help AIDS patients live longer, diagnostic tools such as mammography and ultrasound can help doctors find tumors while they are treatable, and laser surgery techniques have made the most intricate, minute operations routine.

This "toe-to-toe" competition with diseases and disorders is even more remarkable when seen in a historical continuum. An astonishing amount of progress has been made in a very short time. Just two hundred years ago, the existence of germs as a cause of some diseases was unknown. In fact, it was less than 150 years ago that a British surgeon named Joseph Lister had difficulty persuading his fellow doctors that washing their hands before delivering a baby might increase the chances of a healthy delivery (especially if they had just attended to a diseased patient)!

Each book in Lucent's *Diseases and Disorders* series explores a disease or disorder and the knowledge that has been accumulated (or discarded) by doctors through the years. Each book also examines the tools used for pinpointing a diagnosis, as well as the various means that are used to treat or cure a disease. Finally, new ideas are presented—techniques or medicines that may be on the horizon.

Frustration and disappointment are still part of medicine, for not every disease or condition can be cured or prevented. But the limitations of knowledge are being pushed outward constantly; the "most difficult puzzles ever devised" are finding challengers every day.

Introduction

Winning the Battle Against Fear

THE SUBJECT OF breast cancer used to be enveloped in a dark shroud of fear and silence. This often debilitating fear had two dimensions. First, most people—including those who got the disease, their relatives, media reporters, and members of society in general—tended not to talk about it. There seemed to be somewhat of a stigma attached to having breast cancer, as there once was for having *any* kind of cancer. "Cancer was a word that was whispered," says former U.S. First Lady Betty Ford. "People did not talk about it in an open way. If somebody had cancer, and particularly breast cancer, it was a topic that people covered up and only whispered behind their hand so no one would hear it. Cancer was such an unknown."[1] Indeed, ignorance about cancer was widespread. Many women, and men as well, believed (quite erroneously, it turns out) that women who led clean, vigorous lives, ate right and exercised, and otherwise maintained good health did not get breast cancer (or any other form of cancer for that matter). So if a woman did get the disease, the suspicion, usually unspoken, lingered that somehow it must be, at least to some degree, her own fault.

The other major aspect of the fear that long surrounded breast cancer was the widespread perception that getting the disease almost always constituted a death sentence. Typical was the reaction of actress Jill Eikenberry (who starred in the popular TV show *L.A. Law*) when her doctor told her she had breast cancer. "I was devastated," she recalls.

> I was very sure I was going to die. I hadn't ever really known
> anybody who had breast cancer—the only woman I knew who

8

had it was the woman who lived upstairs from my apartment in New York, who had died the year before, leaving three children behind. That was my experience with it. And so I really thought it was a death sentence.[2]

A Real Awakening

Though breast cancer is still a disease to be feared (since it is the most prevalent cancer among women worldwide and the biggest killer of American women in their forties), the once common reactions described above have changed markedly in the past quarter century. On the one hand, society is much more open about cancer, including breast cancer, as well as more sympathetic to those who acquire it. In this regard, a growing number of high-profile women like Betty Ford and Jill Eikenberry have been instrumental in helping to change societal attitudes for the better. (Both women successfully fought and survived the disease.) By courageously speaking out and sharing their personal battles against breast cancer, they have in large degree banished the stigma that once accompanied it. As Ford herself puts it:

Former U.S. Frst Lady Betty Ford greets reporters after her successful surgery for breast cancer at Bethesda Naval Hospital.

It was a real awakening for the women of the United States to have the wife of the president have breast cancer and speak of it. The realization [was], "My heavens, if she can have breast cancer, I can, too. It could happen to me also." There was a tremendous reaction. Immediately women wanted to go for breast examinations to find out if they, too, could possibly have breast cancer. People . . . became more open about addressing the issue.[3]

The rush by many women to get the breast exams that Mrs. Ford describes proved a key element in fighting both the disease and the impression that getting it was an automatic death sentence. Indeed, the array of medical and scientific weapons and approaches to both fighting and preventing the disease have increased in size and quality in the past two decades. Among them are more and better diagnostic tools; more women going for regular checkups and utilizing those tools, and thereby catching the disease in its early stages when it is easier to defeat; advances in various methods of treatment; ongoing research into new and

A radiology technician prepares a 42-year-old woman for a mammogram. Early diagnosis through mammograms is a major factor in fighting breast cancer.

more effective ways to fight breast cancer, including some real hope for the creation of anticancer vaccines; the wide distribution of books, booklets, and fact sheets (especially on the Internet) about the disease; and the creation of numerous support groups for those who get breast cancer and their family members.

An Increase in Survival Rates

The sum total of all of these factors is that more women diagnosed with breast cancer are surviving it and/or living longer than ever before. Between 1960 and 1964, for example, only about 64 percent of women diagnosed with the disease survived for five years. And for those whose cancer ended up spreading to another part of the body, the survival rate was a dismal 7 percent. By 1980 the five-year survival rate for breast cancer had risen to 75 percent; and by the late 1990s, that rate was 85 percent (with 21 percent of those whose cancers had spread surviving).

These figures are certainly encouraging. Yet they represent only a series of small steps in a journey that is far from over. Noted breast cancer specialists Yashar Hirshaut and Peter I. Pressman point out, "As gratifying as this progress has been, we have a long way to go before the fight against breast cancer is fully won. We need the same determination that has taken us this far if we are finally to eradicate this terrible disease."[4] Now that society is finally winning the battle against fear and silence, most researchers, doctors, and breast cancer activists (those who actively urge government and science to do more to fight the disease) believe that the larger battle, too, is winnable. It is no longer a question of *if* breast cancer can be conquered, many say, but *when* this important victory will be achieved.

Chapter 1

Breast Cancer Types, Survival Rates, and Risk Factors

NEXT TO SKIN cancer, breast cancer is the most common kind of cancer among women in the United States. At present, more than 180,000 American women are diagnosed with breast cancer each year, and about 40,000 of these women die from the disease. (Many people are surprised to learn that breast cancer affects men, too, although in far fewer numbers; in the year 2000, for example, about 1,400 American men were diagnosed with breast cancer and roughly 400 of them died.)

For reasons that scientists still cannot explain adequately, the United States has the highest rates of breast cancer in the world. In general, rates of the disease are also high in other developed (industrialized) countries, especially in North America, Australia, and northern and western Europe. By contrast, breast cancer rates and the numbers of deaths caused by the disease are much lower in most of Asia and Africa (with the exception of South Africa). They are lowest of all in China, where only about 12 women per 100,000 get breast cancer (as compared to about 87 women per 100,000 who get it in the United States).

Looking at the world as a whole, rates of the occurrence of breast cancer are rising slightly each year. And experts project that by the year 2010 about 1.35 million new cases of the disease will be

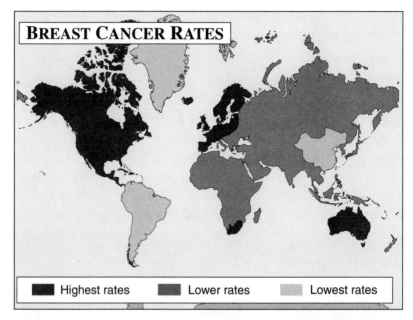

BREAST CANCER RATES

| ■ Highest rates | ■ Lower rates | ▦ Lowest rates |

diagnosed per year. The proportion of these people who will die from breast cancer is unknown, of course. But based on present mortality figures, it could be as high as one in four.

On the one hand, such large numbers of deaths from the disease are sad and frightening, especially for those who are actually diagnosed with it, as well as their relatives and friends. On the other hand, these figures indicate that today a majority of people who are diagnosed with breast cancer do survive. In fact, survival rates for the disease are rising slightly every year, a trend that doctors find encouraging. They cite several major reasons for this trend, most importantly earlier detection and more effective methods of treatment. Only thirty or forty years ago, Dr. Hirshaut and Dr. Pressman explain,

> self-examination was seldom done, and even when women did notice a small lump [in their breast], they may have postponed taking any action out of a combination of ignorance and fear. Therefore, by the time they got to the doctor, they tended to be in later stages of the disease, and that very adversely affected their chances of beating it. Moreover, in the past, the medical profession was much less effective in dealing with the illness than it is now. The

prevailing treatments were, in general, less successful, more disfiguring, and more seriously disruptive of the patient's life.[5]

Regardless of the higher survivor rates, however, breast cancer still kills an unacceptable number of women each year; and the survivors typically must undergo a long and uncertain period of fear and emotional distress; invasive, painful, and sometimes risky treatments; and many lifestyle changes and new ways of thinking about themselves, their loved ones, and life in general. To appreciate the enormity of the toll breast cancer takes on the lives of those who get it and the complex, often difficult steps they must take to become survivors, one must first understand what cancer is, as well as the kinds of breast cancer and the risk factors involved.

What Is Cancer?

Cancer, including that of the breast, consists of clusters of abnormal cells that appear and multiply within a person's body. With some exceptions (such as brain cells), most of the many different kinds of cells in the body divide now and then to produce fresh tissue. The cells that make up the skin are a clear example. About once a month, skin cells divide and the old cells fall away to make way for the new cells. Somehow, in ways scientists do not yet fully understand, the body signals normal cells that it is time to divide and also signals them when it is time to stop dividing.

In the case of cancer cells, by contrast, for some reason the signal to stop dividing does not get through, and the cells go on multiplying. They soon form a cluster, called a tumor, which, more often than not, gets larger and larger until it begins to press on nerves (causing pain) and nearby normal tissues. (Sometimes cells that fail to receive the signal to stop dividing multiply only very slowly and form tumors that prove harmless to the body. These tumors, referred to as benign, or "gentle," are not cancerous; tumors composed of cancer cells are said to be malignant, or "harmful.") Cancerous cells not only grow into malignant tumors, but also invade normal, healthy cells, causing the disease to spread.

A cancerous growth that appears in one part of the body—such as the breast—may stay confined to that area, destroying more and

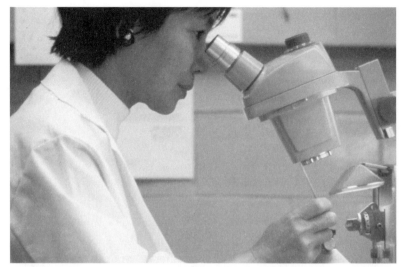

A researcher uses a powerful microscope to study cell abnormalities. Scientists believe that most cancers develop from such abnormalities.

more normal tissue. Sometimes, though, cancer cells from the breast (or another area of the body) can travel to and attack other areas. This deadly formation of new kinds of tumors is called metastasis, the occurrence of which significantly increases the likelihood that the patient will die.

Experts are not sure what causes cancer. But they *are* certain that about 90 percent or more of cancer cases are the result of cellular abnormalities that occur as a result of the normal aging process and/or various environmental factors to which people are exposed. "Just think," medical researcher Marisa Weiss speculates,

> about the many things that might cause the wear and tear that leads to abnormal cell growth—pollutants, hormones, pesticides, smoking, alcohol use, obesity, stress. . . . Or maybe your cells just made a mistake one day when they were making new genes to pass on to their baby cells. Perhaps there was a misprint in the genetic instruction manual that said switch "growth on" instead of "growth off."[6]

(The remainder of cancer cases—somewhat less than 10 percent— are the result of abnormalities in a person's genetic material; this involves inheriting from one's parents a gene or genes that increase the chances of getting cancer.)

The Various Kinds of Breast Cancer

Scientists and doctors categorize or classify the various forms of breast cancer according to what parts of the breast or body these cancers invade. The inside of a normal, healthy breast consists of from fifteen to twenty sections called lobes. Each lobe contains smaller sections called lobules; and each lobule ends in several dozen tiny bulbs that produce milk after a child is born. The lobes, lobules, and milk bulbs in the breast are all linked by tiny tubes known as ducts. The ducts lead to the nipple. The breast also contains numerous blood vessels, as well as narrow tubes, the lymph vessels, which connect to small oval-shaped organs called lymph nodes, located to the sides of the breasts under the arms, and in the chest. (The lymph nodes and vessels, which exist throughout the

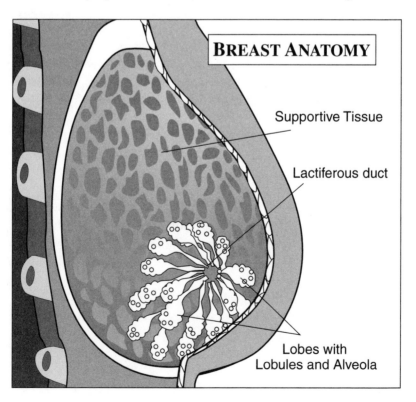

body and carry a clear fluid called lymph, remove bacteria from the blood and also circulate protective white blood cells.)

Unfortunately breast cancer can strike any and all of these normal sections of the breast and lymph system (as well as other parts of the body). Most cases of breast cancer occur in the breast ducts, in which case doctors call them ductal (or duct cell) carcinoma. If the cancer stays confined to the duct, it is referred to as ductal carcinoma in situ (DCIS). (The Latin term *in situ* means "in its place," in this case denoting that the cancer stays in its original site.) In situ cancers are also said to be noninvasive because they do not invade other areas of the breast. By contrast, if the ductal cancer grows beyond the duct and invades the nearby tissue, doctors call it invasive (or infiltrating) ductal carcinoma (IDC).

The same terms (i.e., carcinoma, in situ, and invasive) are used to describe cancers that grow in the lobes of the breast. If the cancer stays confined to the lobular area, it is called lobular carcinoma in situ (LCIS); whereas if it goes beyond the lobes and attacks neighboring tissue, doctors label it invasive lobular carcinoma (ILC).

In general, the malignant tumors of these most common kinds of breast cancer are irregular in shape and firm to the touch. Doctors classify some rarer types of breast cancer by separate names because their tumors look different under a microscope. Tubular breast cancer, for example, is so named because the cancer cells look like little tubes. And medullary carcinoma is named after the medulla, a section of the brain, because this kind of tumor is the same color as brain tissue. Papillary carcinoma features cells that stick out like little fingers; and Paget's disease affects the nipple and the tissue surrounding it. Doctors emphasize that these less common kinds of breast cancer are more easily treatable and account for far fewer deaths than IDC or ILC.

On the other hand, the chance of dying of breast cancer increases significantly if the malignant cells spread beyond the breast itself. As the National Institutes of Health (NIH) explains in its official, regularly updated booklet on breast cancer:

> When cancer arises in breast tissue and spreads (metastasizes) outside the breast, cancer cells are often found in the lymph

nodes under the arm. . . . If the cancer has reached these nodes, it means that cancer cells may have spread to other parts of the body—other lymph nodes and other organs, such as the bones, liver, or lungs. When cancer spreads from its original location to another part of the body, the new tumor has the same kind of abnormal cells and the same name as the primary tumor. For example, if breast cancer spreads to the brain, the cancer cells in the brain are actually breast cancer cells. The disease is called metastatic breast cancer. (It is not brain cancer.) Doctors sometimes call this "distant" disease.[7]

Causes and Risk Factors

As for what causes these various kinds of breast cancer, scientists and doctors are as uncertain as they are for the causes of cancer in general. However, numerous studies of breast cancer patients and their habits and environments have been conducted over the past few decades. And these studies point to certain behaviors, exposures to certain kinds of materials, and other factors that experts call risk factors. In other words, evidence shows that a person's risk of getting breast cancer increases when she or he encounters

These human breast cancer cells have metastasized and invaded the lymph nodes. Physicians sometimes call metastasis "distant disease."

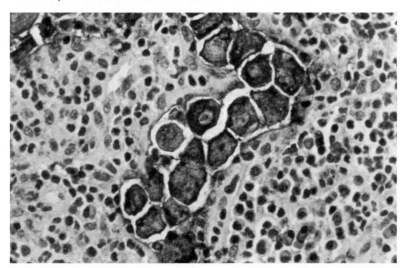

such factors. (This does not mean that any single one of these factors is the cause of the person's cancer, i.e., that it causes her or his cells to grow abnormally; this may happen as a result of diverse and varying combinations of factors.)

Researchers try to identify risk factors to find out who is most likely to get a certain disease, as well as to discern the cause or causes of the disease so that preventive measures and/or a cure might be found. Great strides have been made in such research in certain areas. For example, smoking has been shown to be a risk factor for lung cancer; and high cholesterol increases one's risk of getting heart disease. Scientists usually determine such risk factors by looking at a large number of people—often from one to two thousand or more—and identifying various features about them. The researchers determine who gets a certain disease and then try to find a connection between the disease and the features that commonly occur within the group. At times, as in the case of lung cancer and smoking, risk factors can be dramatic, making it quite clear that avoiding a certain behavior will lessen an individual's likelihood of getting a disease.

In the case of breast cancer, however, nothing as dramatic as the connections between cholesterol and heart disease and between smoking and lung cancer have yet been found. As Susan Love, one of the world's leading experts on breast cancer, puts it:

> With breast cancer, the sad reality is that we can't say, as with lung cancer, "You're fairly safe because you're not in this particular population [group that engages in a certain behavior]." In fact, 70 percent of breast cancer patients have none of the classical risk factors in their background. . . . It would be much more convenient if we could say, "This causes breast cancer, so don't do it." But breast cancer is what is known as a "multifactorial disease"—that is, it has many causes which interact with each other in ways we don't understand yet.[8]

Even though a majority of women diagnosed with breast cancer do not have the most common risk factors, hundreds of thousands of women who get the disease *do* have these factors. So it is important for all women to be aware of them. This extra knowledge can definitely be beneficial, but in some cases it can also be a little scary for the layperson. Dr. Love adds the following cautionary advice for women educating themselves about the risk factors:

> Overestimating the importance of risk factors can cause needless mental anguish if you have one of them in your background. On the other hand, you may create a false sense of security if you don't have them. I can't count the number of times patients have come in to me with a suspicious lump that turns out to be malignant and, stunned, say, "I don't know how this happened! No one in my family ever had breast cancer!" I tell them they are in good company—most breast cancer patients don't have a family history of breast cancer. By virtue of being women, we are at risk for breast cancer.[9]

Some General and Specific Risk Factors

Doctors recognize several risk factors for breast cancer, some of a general nature (which are pretty much impossible to avoid) and others more specific (which can sometimes be avoided). The most general risk factor of all is age. The disease is uncommon (though certainly does occur at times) in women under the age of thirty-five, while the risk increases considerably for women over age fifty and especially for those over sixty. Also, for reasons unknown, breast cancer strikes a higher percentage of white women than African American or Asian women. Another general factor is family history. Though, as Dr. Love points out, a woman with no family history can get the disease, there is no doubt that women whose mothers, sisters, or daughters have had breast cancer are more susceptible to getting it. (These are called first-degree relatives; a person's grandmothers, aunts, cousins, and so forth are second-degree relatives, whose breast cancers, if any, represent a lower risk factor for that person.) In addition, and not surprisingly, a woman who has had cancer in one of her breasts has a higher risk of getting it in the other breast.

An example of a somewhat more specific risk factor is the amount of estrogen (an important female hormone) a woman is exposed to and for how long. According to the NIH:

Middle-aged women, like the one pictured here, are more likely to get breast cancer because they have been exposed to estrogen longer than young women have.

Evidence suggests that the longer a woman is exposed to estrogen (estrogen made by the body, taken as a drug, or delivered by a patch), the more likely she is to develop breast cancer. For example, the risk is somewhat increased among women who began menstruation at an early age (before age 12), experienced menopause late (after age 55), never had children, or took hormone replacement therapy for long periods of time. Each of these factors increases the amount of time a woman's body is exposed to estrogen.[10]

A more specific, and perhaps more obvious, risk factor for breast cancer is exposure to higher-than-normal doses of certain kinds of radiation (usually a potentially harmful variety called ionizing radiation). The most extreme cases, of course, are the victims of the atomic bombs dropped on Japan in 1945 and the Chernobyl nuclear accident (in Ukraine) in 1986. The rates of many kinds of cancer, including breast cancer, increased significantly in those exposed to the radiation in these disasters. On a lesser scale, people who are constantly exposed to small doses of radiation as part of treatment for various diseases and conditions (such as radiation treatment for skin cancer) are slightly more at risk for breast cancer than those who do not receive such treatments. Evidence also suggests that breasts that are undergoing a burst of development are more at risk from such radiation than mature breasts. So the highest radiation risk factor is for the breasts of a fetus or of a young woman undergoing puberty (when her breasts are rapidly developing).

Is Diet a Risk Factor?

One of the most talked-about and controversial risk factors for breast cancer is diet. The question is whether what people eat can promote—or conversely, deter—the incidence of the disease. Doctors disagree considerably on this subject. But it is safe to say that most of them agree that a low-fat, high-fiber diet *may* reduce one's risk of getting breast cancer.

The reasons for this, if it is indeed true, are not completely understood. But researchers suspect that it may be related to the fact that the higher a person's intake of fat, the more estrogen circulates through the person's body; and high exposure to estrogen is a known risk factor for the disease. A recent study done by the American Health Foundation (in New York City) looked at the daily intake of fat by large numbers of women. Those who lowered their fat intake from 38 percent of their total calories per day (the average for women in the United States) to 20 percent also lowered their levels of estrogen.

It is important to emphasize that no one has yet shown conclusively that lowering daily fat intake and other dietary habits and factors actually reduce the risk of breast cancer. However, some powerful recent evidence suggests that this may indeed be the case. A number of researchers have studied (and continue to study) Japanese women. Of all the developed countries, Japan is the only one with very low breast cancer rates. Only 22 in every

This woman eating an apple may have good reason for smiling. Researchers suspect that fruits and vegetables, many of which are rich in fiber, may offer some protection against breast cancer.

100,000 Japanese women get the disease (compared to 87 in every 100,000 in the United States). Deborah Axelrod asks, "Why is there significantly *less* breast cancer in Japan?" and answers:

> Japanese women tend to eat significantly less fat than American women do, and they also eat a relatively large quantity of estrogenic plant-based foods like soy. . . . In simple terms, soy and other plant-based estrogenic foods may—I repeat *may*—offer a certain degree of protection against breast cancer. As for the low-fat diet . . . the ratio of fats in the Japanese diet has been used as a model for a number of American studies. . . . The theory is that American women may be hurting themselves in two ways at once. [In addition to increasing estrogen levels, a high-fat diet has less fiber.] Think about it: if you're eating eggs and bacon for breakfast, you usually aren't eating cereal and berries [which are rich in fiber]. This relative lack of fiber in the American diet may also play a role in promoting breast cancer. The jury is still out on the question. But it continues to interest

many scientists around the world, and we hope to have more definitive answers on the subject in coming years.[11]

For the moment, the jury, as Dr. Axelrod puts it, is still out on many of the risk factors for breast cancer. For the most part, therefore, it is unclear what preventive behaviors people should adopt to decrease their risk of getting the disease. However, virtually all doctors advocate avoiding exposure to harmful kinds of radiation, limiting fat and increasing fiber in the diet, and doing regular exercise. A healthy person has a better chance of fighting and defeating various diseases, including cancer.

Chapter 2

Screening for and Diagnosing Breast Cancer

WHATEVER ONE'S RISK factors for breast cancer might be, the best general approach to dealing with the potential onset of the disease is early detection. Part of the overall process of diagnosing the disease, detecting a tumor early—before it has had a chance to invade nearby healthy tissue—has proven time and again to be a key factor in successfully fighting and defeating breast cancer.

Both women and their physicians play important roles in detecting the presence of the disease. At least by age twenty, all women

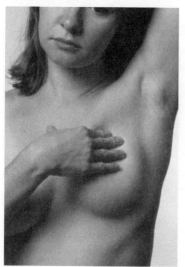

should educate themselves about the warning signs of breast cancer, be vigilant for them, and immediately report them to their doctor and get an official diagnosis. They should also perform regular self-exams of their breasts, looking for small lumps that they have not noticed before. Yet it is important to emphasize that many women do not display the classic warning

A young woman examines her breast. Self-exams can sometimes detect breast cancer in its early stages.

25

signs of the disease; and self-exams are far from foolproof, even for women who perform them correctly and regularly.

More effective are regular exams by a medical doctor, which should begin when a woman starts seeing a gynecologist (most often in her late teens or early twenties). This is part of a process known as screening, in which doctors examine healthy people with no symptoms of breast cancer in hopes of detecting the disease in its early stages when it is most treatable.

Eventually, as a woman ages, the screening process also includes a mammogram, the best, most sensitive test presently used to screen for breast cancer. Essentially, a mammogram is an X ray of the breast. It can detect some tumors before they are large enough for women and their doctors to feel them. Most doctors presently advise that women get an initial, or baseline, mammogram at age thirty-five; and beginning at age forty, they should be screened once a year. (The exception is women who have a strong family history of breast cancer, especially among first-degree relatives; these women should begin yearly screening earlier than age forty and should consult their doctors to determine just how much earlier.)

Today, the standard method of administering mammograms is to take two images of each breast, one horizontal, the other diagonal.

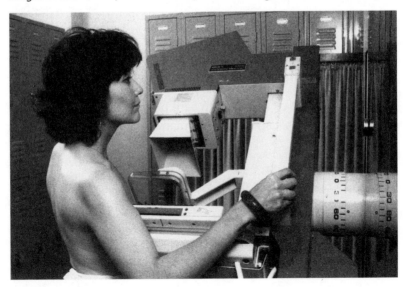

Warning Signs and Self-Exams

A doctor will order one or more of these diagnostic tests, depending on how sure or unsure he or she might be about whether a suspicious lump is benign or malignant. But before the doctor and patient reach this stage in the diagnosis process, someone must detect the suspicious lump in the first place. The doctor him- or herself might feel the lump when examining a woman's breast; or the lump may show up in a mammogram.

Quite often, however, both patient and doctor are alerted to the presence of a potential breast tumor by the patient's own vigilance. First, a woman may notice one or more of the warning or trouble signs of the disease (which may or may not be present). According to the American Cancer Society, these can include

> a generalized swelling of part of a breast (even if no distinct lump is felt), skin irritation or dimpling, nipple pain or retraction (turning inward), redness or scaliness of the nipple or breast skin, or a discharge other than breast milk [from the nipple]. Sometimes a breast cancer can spread to underarm lymph nodes that are obviously enlarged, even before the original tumor in the breast tissue is large enough to be felt.[12]

Most women who get breast cancer do not show these particular symptoms, the more common warning sign being a new lump or mass within the breast. "A mass that is painless, hard, and has irregular edges is more likely to be cancerous," says the American Cancer Society, "but some rare cancers are tender, soft, and rounded. For this reason, it is important that any new breast mass or lump be checked by a health care provider with experience in diagnosis of breast cancer."[13] A woman may discover such a lump simply by chance or through a self-exam, which most doctors advise doing about once a month. The American Cancer Society provides (both in booklets and on the Internet) step-by-step instructions in doing such an exam, as do a number of helpful books presently on the market. Also, of course, one's doctor or an experienced nurse can provide the necessary instruction.

There is presently a sharp difference of opinion among medical professionals about the worth of breast self-exams. Some, like Susan

Love, suggest that such exams do not detect cancerous lumps any more reliably than regular screening by mammograms. "[The] benefits [of self-exams] are psychological," she says, and "probably won't make a difference in your physical health."[14] By contrast, Hirshaut and Pressman, speaking for a large proportion of doctors, strongly advocate self-exam, saying, "The procedure is simple. It is free. It can be done on a regular basis. It is not dangerous. It is the way most breast lumps are found."[15]

Indeed, numerous women have discovered breast tumors on their own. "I found the lump myself," says famous cooking

The virtues of early detection are illustrated by the longevity of cooking expert Julia Child. Through a self-exam, she caught her breast cancer in time.

guru Julia Child, who had breast cancer in the 1960s and managed to beat the disease because she caught it in time. "It was about the size of a lima bean," she recalls. "I could feel it very definitely. . . . [Now] I do self-examination monthly and have a mammogram every year." For those women who, like Child, perform regular self-exams and do happen to find a suspicious lump, it is crucial to see a doctor immediately. As she bluntly puts it, "You're just stupid if you don't go to the doctor. It's up to you to take care of yourself, not up to anyone else."[16]

Getting a Mammogram

Whatever the ultimate reliability of breast self-exams may be, the fact is that large numbers of women do not perform them regularly. And a good many cases of breast cancer end up being detected in mammograms during routine screening for the disease. Mammograms are most often done at the office of a radiologist (a doctor who specializes in using X rays and other forms of radiation to diagnose and treat disease), a breast screening center, a hospital, or a physicians' group practice.

When a woman goes to one of these places for a routine mammogram, an X-ray technician takes a two-dimensional black-and-white picture of the inside of each of her breasts. First, the patient removes all of her clothing from the waist up and stands or sits in an upright position (since the X-ray machine is a vertical structure). She leans forward and raises her arms to specific positions so that the X-ray machine has a clear view of the breast. The machine is then adjusted so that the breast is firmly compressed between two surfaces—the platform and compression plate. The technician places an X-ray plate under the breast for the first picture, then puts it on the side of the breast for the next picture. The patient must stay perfectly still and hold her breath while the picture is taken. Next, the technician and patient repeat the same procedure for the other breast. The pressure on the breast from its contact with the compression plate is sometimes a bit uncomfortable, but it should not be painful. If it *is* painful, the technician stops and repositions the patient.

The image at left shows the interior of a normal breast. The other image clearly shows a cancerous tumor, diagnosed as colloid carcinoma.

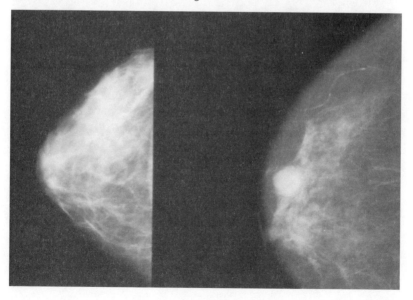

When the X-ray film is developed, a radiologist or other specially trained individual reads the pictures and determines if any suspicious-looking lumps exist in the breast tissues. It is essential that the person be highly qualified because such X-ray pictures can be difficult to interpret. This is partly because cancer and benign lumps have the same density as breast tissue; and if the patient has a white lump in the middle of some dense tissue, it will not be obvious on the mammogram, since the tissue will hide it. Moreover, a

Radiologists are experts trained to read and interpret X rays. This radiologist examines an X ray of a breast to determine if any suspicious lumps are visible.

number of benign conditions can look the same as cancer on a mammogram. Scarring or fat necrosis (dead fat), for instance, can look suspicious to a doctor reading a mammogram. And so can a noncancerous lesion known as a radial scar. In fact, a radial scar can be hard to diagnose even under the microscope, and an expert breast pathologist must often be consulted to be sure no cancer is present.

Not a Perfect Science

Such difficulties raise an extremely important point about diagnosing breast cancer through mammograms (as well as through other imaging techniques). Although mammography is the most sensitive tool for detecting early breast cancers and pinpoints them most of time, it is not a perfect science. Both false negatives (when a mammogram appears normal even though a breast cancer tumor is actually present) and false positives (when a mammogram reads an abnormality but it later turns out that no cancer is actually present) are fairly routine occurrences. The National Cancer Institute estimates that an average of 20 percent of mammograms will read false negative, while about 5 to 10 percent will read false positive. In general, false negatives occur more often in younger women than in older women. Younger women usually have denser breasts that contain many glands and ligaments, which make breast cancers more difficult to identify in mammograms. In older women, by contrast, breast tissues become more fatty and breast cancers are more easily identified in mammograms. False positives are also more common in younger women. According to the National Cancer Institute, about 30 percent of women ages 40 to 49 have a false-positive mammogram, as compared with about 25 percent for women age 50 and older.

Naturally, receiving either a false-negative or false-positive diagnosis can cause the patient a considerable amount of anxiety. At least in the case of a false positive, the ultimate outcome itself is positive—that is, the person turns out not to have breast cancer. For a woman who receives a false negative, by contrast, the consequences can be emotionally devastating.

Most women who go for routine screenings once a year do not suspect there is anything wrong with their breasts. But sometimes a woman insists either that she has felt a small suspicious lump or that somehow she can sense—call it a "gut" feeling—that something is wrong. If the woman does not feel right with the diagnosis, she should insist on further tests. "If you think something is wrong," says a breast cancer survivor named Leanne,

> don't let a doctor tell you there's not. Don't let him say you're just a tired housewife or whatever, because if your body is telling you something, you need to listen even if it takes going to ten doctors in a row. I knew something was wrong, and everybody kept telling me, "You're fine, you're fine," and eventually I let them convince me.[17]

Other Initial Detection Methods

Considering that mammograms do not detect breast cancers 100 percent of the time, scientists are working diligently on improving diagnostic techniques. Various versions of a digital (i.e., computerized) mammogram are under development. One was approved by the federal Food and Drug Administration (FDA) in January 2000. Its advantages are that it allows easier correction of under- or overexposures that can happen with regular X-ray films; it can "see" better through tissues of varying densities; and it stores its images electronically, so that they can be sent quickly to radiologists or other specialists situated far away. So far, however, the digital versions have not proven to be any more accurate overall than the normal X-ray versions. Efforts are also under way to find ways to detect early breast cancers by finding "markers," chemical or other signs of the disease, in the blood, urine, or secretions from the nipples.

For the moment, however, the main supplemental screening test used to back up regular mammograms (before the more invasive biopsy is done) is a sonogram, or ultrasound. Perhaps the most familiar use of sonograms is to view the fetus within the womb of a pregnant mother. In the case of a breast sonogram, the doctor or a trained technician moves an instrument called a transducer across the surface of the breast. The transducer sends short pulses of sound through the breast tissue; if they strike something solid, they bounce back to a screen, which records them and produces an image.

Unfortunately, so far sonograms have not proven to be sensitive enough to pick up very tiny lumps, as mammograms can; so they are not as effective as mammograms as general screening tools. However, a sonogram *is* useful for confirming the existence of a lump that a woman and her doctor can feel but that does not show up on a mammogram. If the lump is only a fluid-filled cyst, the sound waves will pass right through it; whereas if the lump is a solid mass, and therefore potentially a cancer, the waves will bounce back.

In addition to sonograms, MRIs are increasingly used as a supplement to mammography. An MRI (which stands for "magnetic resonance imaging") uses a strong magnetic field to see inside the body. A computer measures and analyzes the field and creates a detailed image that the doctor can study on a screen. MRI technology shows tremendous promise for the future of fighting breast

The tremendous potential of MRI technology for spotting early breast cancers is apparent in this comparison of a standard x-ray and an MRI image.

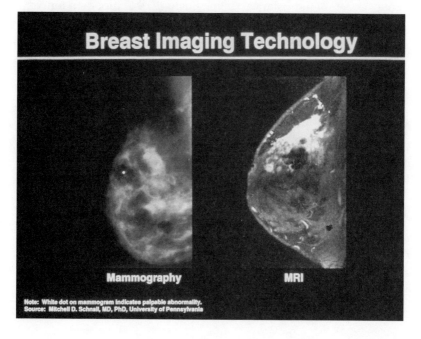

Breast Imaging Technology

Mammography

MRI

Note: White dot on mammogram indicates palpable abnormality.
Source: Mitchell D. Schnall, MD, PhD, University of Pennsylvania

cancer, as outlined by Carol B. Stelling, of the University of Texas M. D. Anderson Cancer Center:

> Several potential applications of breast MRI may increase our ability to visualize the disease: assisting in detection and diagnosis for women at high risk for breast cancer with hard-to-interpret mammograms; clarifying how much breast tissue is involved to aid in treatment planning for women with known cancer . . . and detecting recurrent cancer in the breast after breast-conserving therapy and/or . . . breast implants or reconstructive surgery.[18]

For the moment, however, MRI images, like sonograms, do not "see" tiny tumors that are more often revealed by mammograms. So MRI technology remains experimental and merely supplementary in breast cancer screening.

Another up-and-coming imaging method, the PET scan (positron-emission tomography) detects and takes pictures of radiation given off by materials circulating within the body. Using a needle, a doctor or nurse injects the patient with a substance that gives off a mild form of radiation. The patient then lies down for a while to let the substance travel through the bloodstream and reach the breasts. The PET scanner takes pictures of the breasts from various angles, and a computer shows these images in color on a screen. The main advantage of the PET scan is that it *may* detect cancerous tumors that do not show up using other techniques, especially lumps in the lymph nodes. However, PET scans are not yet nearly as reliable overall as mammograms are in general screening for breast cancer.

The Final Step—Biopsy

Once the initial screening for breast cancer is accomplished and assuming a suspicious lump has been found, the next step is usually a biopsy. A biopsy is necessary for an absolutely certain diagnosis, as Hirshaut and Pressman explain:

> An experienced doctor often knows by its "feel" what a lump is, and after a mammogram, he may be able to quite accurately predict whether a tumor or thickening in the breast is malig-

nant or not. That educated hunch, however, is not enough to go on. The final diagnosis of breast cancer depends on an examination of the suspicious tissue under a microscope.[19]

The American Cancer Society strongly concurs, saying, "A biopsy is the only way to tell if cancer is really present."[20]

Several types of biopsy are performed in breast cancer diagnosis, depending on the situation. One of the most common and least painful types is the fine needle aspiration biopsy (FNAB), which employs a thinner needle than the kind used in blood tests. The doctor might guide the needle into the lump while he or she feels or holds the lump with the fingers. If the lump cannot be felt easily enough, the doctor can do a sonogram and watch the screen, which will show the exact position of both the lump and needle. Once the needle enters the lump, the doctor draws out some material. If it is perfectly clear fluid, the lump is most likely a benign

---

One effective method of biopsy, shown here, utilizes a digital X ray camera, which projects an image of the patient's breast on a screen. The image guides the insertion of the biopsy needle.

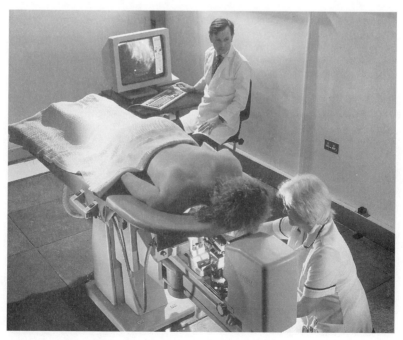

cyst. Bloody or cloudy fluid could mean either a benign cyst or, on rare occasions, cancer. If solid tissue particles are drawn out through the needle, the chances of the lump being cancerous are a good deal higher. In *all cases*, though, the doctor sends the material to a lab to be examined under a microscope. If any questions or uncertainties exist after that examination, a doctor will recommend, and indeed the patient should insist on, having another kind of biopsy to make a more precise diagnosis.

The remaining forms of biopsy get progressively more invasive because they consist of attempts to retrieve a larger tissue sample for inspection. A core needle biopsy, for example, uses a thicker needle and removes a cylinder of tissue from $1/16$ to $1/8$ of an inch in diameter and about half an inch long from the breast lump. In some cases, the doctor may feel that a full surgical biopsy should be done. In such a procedure, part or all of the lump is removed. (If only some of the tumor is taken out, it is called an incisional biopsy; if the whole tumor is removed, doctors call it an excisional biopsy.) Surgical biopsies are most commonly done in a hospital

A doctor performs a surgical biopsy, hoping to discover the exact nature of a patient's solid tumor.

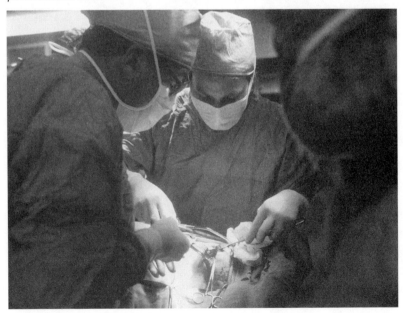

outpatient department under a local anesthesia (which numbs the breast but does not render the patient unconscious).

Once the tissue removed in a biopsy is examined under a microscope by an expert, the diagnosis stage is complete. Of the two main possible outcomes, of course, one is good, the other bad; and if it is bad, the patient and doctor must start discussing treatment options. According to the American Cancer Society, if the diagnosis is a benign condition, no further treatment is needed. On the other hand, if the diagnosis reveals cancer, the woman has time to learn about the disease and to discuss the various available treatment options with her cancer care team, friends, and family. The short delay until treatment does no harm.

Chapter 3

Local Treatments for Breast Cancer

IF AND WHEN, after a thorough diagnosis, a woman receives the distressing news that her breast lump is malignant, the next step is treatment. Today many different treatments exist for breast cancer. And choosing the right or appropriate treatment for any single woman depends on numerous factors. Among these are her age, her general health, whether she is pre- or post-menopausal (i.e., if she still gets her period or no longer gets it), the size of her breasts, and her mental and emotional attitude toward her condition.

In most cases, the most important consideration for the patient and her doctor in choosing a treatment is the "stage" of the breast cancer. The disease usually gets progressively worse if left untreated. And a cancer in its earlier stages responds better to certain treatments, while these treatments may not work as well for a tumor in more advanced stages, when it may have to be treated more aggressively.

Doctors usually break down the staging of breast cancer into five general categories or levels (designated in Roman numerals). Stage 0 consists of very early tumors, such as LCIS and DCIS, that are still in situ, or localized to a lobe or duct in the breast. In such cases, the cancer cells have not yet invaded nearby tissues. In Stage I, the cancer *has* begun to invade nearby tissues, but the tumor remains no more than an inch across and appears not to have spread beyond the breast. Stage II includes tumors that are still less than an inch across but have spread to the lymph nodes under the arms, tumors that are between one and two inches across that may or may not have spread to the lymph nodes, and tumors more than two inches across that have not spread to the lymph nodes. In Stage III (sometimes called locally advanced cancer), the cancerous mass is more than two inches across and has spread to the underarm lymph nodes or to other lymph nodes. Finally, Stage IV breast cancer involves metastasis, in which the disease has spread beyond the breast and nearby lymph nodes to other parts of the body.

The doctor and other members of a woman's cancer care team may recommend one or perhaps a combination of specific treatments, depending on the stage of the disease. Overall, these treatments are of two basic types—local and systemic. Local treatments, which are covered in this chapter, involve or concentrate primarily on the breast containing the cancer. They include removal surgery (both lumpectomy—removing only the lump itself; and mastectomy—removing most or all of the breast), reconstructive surgery, and radiation treatment. Some degree of

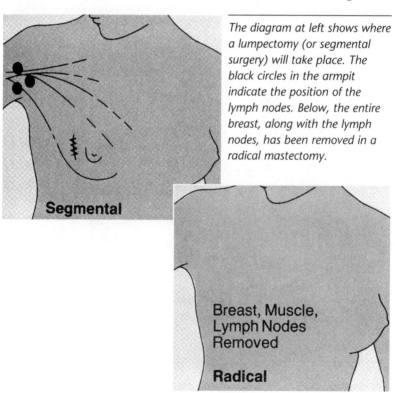

The diagram at left shows where a lumpectomy (or segmental surgery) will take place. The black circles in the armpit indicate the position of the lymph nodes. Below, the entire breast, along with the lymph nodes, has been removed in a radical mastectomy.

Segmental

Breast, Muscle, Lymph Nodes Removed

Radical

radiation treatment is almost always used as a follow-up to surgery to destroy any stray cancer cells the surgery may have missed. (Systemic treatments, which involve the whole body, are sometimes used in conjunction with local treatments, depending on the situation.)

Choosing a Lumpectomy

The first local treatment women and doctors usually consider is surgery, either a lumpectomy or mastectomy. More often than not, because they are still relatively small, Stage 0 and Stage I tumors (and sometimes Stage II tumors) can be treated by a lumpectomy rather than the more drastic option of mastectomy. "The smaller the tumor, the greater your options," says physician Thomas G. Frazier. "A lot of people have this fear that they're going to lose their breast, and that's just not true anymore."[21]

The fear to which Dr. Frazier refers is based on the way the disease was often handled in the past. A few decades ago, full mastectomy was much more common than lumpectomy because doctors knew less about breast cancer and how it spreads; and most surgeons thought it better to be on the safe side and just remove the whole breast. Luckily, many women today can safely opt for a lumpectomy. According to Deborah Axelrod:

> Many women, and some doctors, still cling to the old belief that more is better—that is, taking more of the breast away will increase your chance of survival. This simply is not true. Studies have shown that the lumpectomy procedure produces an equivalent survival rate to full removal of the breast. So the first thing to remember in making this big decision is that the breast-sparing choice is an equally safe one. I always remind women, furthermore, that while I cannot tape on a breast that has been removed, you can always go back for *more* surgery if for any reason the lumpectomy procedure is not successful. Most women never come back for more.[22]

Still, lumpectomy is not appropriate for everyone. Doctors will generally rule out the procedure, even for those women with fairly small tumors, under certain conditions. These include (among

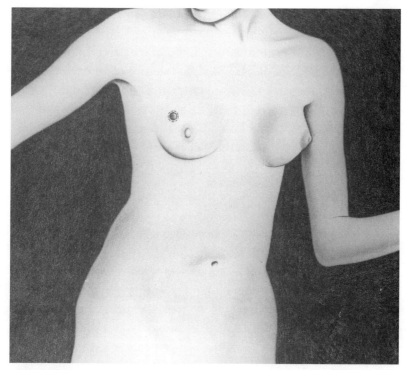

Lumps like the one pictured on this woman's right breast are routinely removed in lumpectomies (or wide excisions).

others) the presence of two or more tumors in the same breast, the reappearance of cancerous cells in the area of a lumpectomy after repeated surgeries, and pregnancy of the patient (since the radiation used to follow up the surgery may harm the fetus).

As for the procedure itself, the average lumpectomy (also called a wide excision) consists of removing the malignant mass, along with roughly three-quarters of an inch (two centimeters) of healthy tissue from all around the tumor. Removing this small amount of healthy tissue is a safety measure to make sure no cancerous cells are left in the region of the former lump. In almost all cases, the surgeon also removes a few of the nearby lymph nodes (which medical professionals examine afterward). This is done to make sure that no cancer has spread to the nodes and therefore to provide the patient with a more accurate prognosis (forecast of the outcome of the surgery; in other words, whether it looks like a complete success or whether further surgery or other forms of treatment seem warranted).

Today most lumpectomies are ambulatory procedures, that is, the patient is allowed to go home on the same day of her operation. On the one hand, this is good for the patient. She can feel a psychological lift knowing that her surgery was routine and uncomplicated; and she can look forward to recuperating in the familiar, comfortable surroundings of her own home. On the other hand, Dr. Axelrod points out:

> Sometimes loved ones fail to recognize the seriousness of this treatment for breast cancer and don't give the kind of support and attention many women need afterward. They simply assume that if you can get home in a few hours, things must not be so dire. This is just one of countless reasons why it's so important to communicate with your closest support system, be that a spouse or partner, adult children, friends, or anyone else whose support you expect after surgery.[23]

Choosing a Mastectomy

Unfortunately, sometimes various factors rule out a lumpectomy, and a mastectomy is the only way to remove the breast cancer cleanly and save the patient's life. Stage III and IV breast cancers (and some Stage II cancers) often warrant a mastectomy. The question is how extensive and invasive the procedure will be, since modern surgeons perform several kinds of mastectomies, depending on their patients' individual circumstances. If the tumor's size and location allow the surgeon to save part of the breast, he or she will perform a partial (or segmental) mastectomy. In this procedure, according to the NIH, "the surgeon removes the cancer, some of the breast tissue, the lining over the chest muscles below the tumor, and usually some of the lymph nodes under the arm. In most cases, radiation therapy follows."[24]

The other forms of mastectomy include total (or simple) mastectomy, in which the surgeon removes the entire breast and some of the underarm lymph nodes; modified radical mastectomy, in which the breast, some underarm lymph nodes, the lining over the

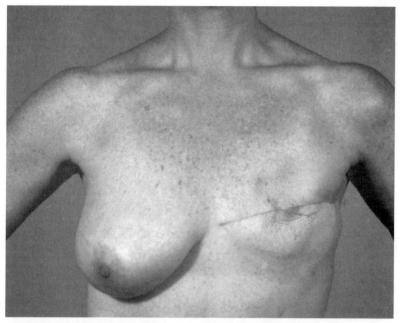

This woman's left breast has been removed in a mastectomy

chest muscles, and sometimes some of the muscles in the chest wall are removed; and radical mastectomy, in which the surgeon removes the breast, all underarm lymph nodes, and all the chest muscles beneath the breast. (Although radical mastectomy used to be the norm, today surgeons resort to it only when the cancer has spread to the chest muscles themselves.) These more extensive and invasive forms of mastectomy may be needed if the cancer has spread to various parts of the breast and/or the underarm lymph nodes. But full mastectomies (except for radical ones) may be indicated for other reasons. The breast may be so small in comparison to the tumor itself that a lumpectomy would leave almost no tissue or a deformed breast. Or the patient may, for various reasons (for example, inability to get to a treatment center on a regular basis or flat-out refusal), not have follow-up radiation treatment, in which case more breast tissue must be taken as a safety measure. Also, as happens in a few cases, the patient may insist on a full mastectomy, fearing that a lumpectomy or partial mastectomy will fail to get all the cancer.

Some women go further and opt for *double* mastectomies, even though one breast appears to be cancer-free. Those patients who make this extremely difficult choice are usually very fearful about the possibility of getting cancer in the healthy breast; so they decide on a double mastectomy for peace of mind, as well as to be on the safe side. "I had a double mastectomy (my choice) to be sure it [the cancer] wouldn't recur in the other breast," says Susan, a mother of four. "My husband and I had done some research . . . dissected all the words of my diagnosis and decided this would give me some sense of security."[25]

Susan's surgery was successful. Indeed, mastectomies, supplemented by radiation and other forms of treatment, are more often than not highly effective and leave the patient cancer-free. However, like all kinds of surgery, mastectomies can sometimes have unpleasant side effects (besides routine potential surgical side effects, such as bleeding from the incision, slow healing, and the risk of infection). For example, removal of the breast can cause a woman's weight to become imbalanced, particularly if she has large breasts. Such an imbalance can make the neck and back feel uncomfortable. In addition, the skin in the area of the removed breast may be tight, or the arm and shoulder muscles may feel stiff. During surgery nerves may be injured or cut, so some women report feeling a slight numbness and tingling in the chest, underarm, shoulder, and/or upper arm. Such feelings usually disappear after a few weeks or months. However, some women end up with permanent numbness in one or two spots. Also, the removal of the lymph nodes under the arm naturally impedes the flow of lymph through that area of a woman's body. Some women find to their dismay that this fluid collects in the arm and hand, causing a kind of swelling known as lymphedema. At present no cure exists for lymphedema; but exercise, proper diet, and other therapies can significantly reduce the swelling.

Postsurgery Experiences

As might be expected, patients' immediate reactions to breast surgery vary from person to person. Some experience little difficulty during recovery and adjust well to the loss of a breast. "I was

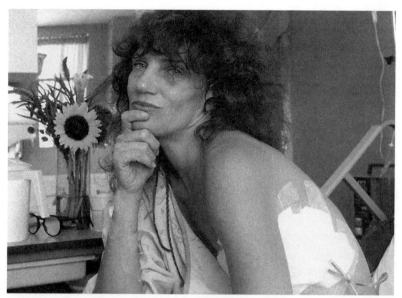

A woman who has just undergone a mastectomy of her left breast tries to put her situation in perspective. Some women feel fortunate that they did not lose a leg or an arm instead.

struck by how nonintrusive [not disruptive of her bodily functions and life] the surgery had been," recalls Victoria, who had a mastectomy.

> It [reminded me of] how superfluous [extra and nonessential] these breasts really are. I remember feeling after the surgery how lucky I was that it wasn't an arm or leg or something I needed to be who I was. The loss didn't have any effect on me. I could do what I had always done.[26]

In contrast, other women who undergo a mastectomy may experience considerable discomfort in the days following surgery. This is mainly true for those who must be fitted with "drains," small tubes that carry away excess fluid that can build up under the skin in the breast area. Most often the drains remain in place from one to five days (although occasionally longer). "Without a doubt, the major complaint from women [who have had mastectomies] about the physical part of the surgery are the drains," writes Kathy LaTour, secretary of the National Coalition for Cancer Survivorship and herself a breast cancer survivor. "The nurses empty them while you are in the hospital and then you will take them home with you and learn to drain them yourself. They don't hurt. They are just inconvenient and a constant fuss."[27] Joyce, who had to endure her drains longer than most mastectomy patients, remembers that she "was in the hospital nine days and came home with all kinds of tubes and hated it, hated it, hated it. This was horrible. That was probably the most debilitating, dehumanizing, degrading thing that I can remember."[28]

Compensating for the Loss of a Breast

Over the longer term, of course, a woman who has undergone a mastectomy must face the fact that her breast is now partially or completely missing. A number of women find this very disturbing and some actually grieve the loss. According to the National Cancer Institute, mastectomy patients generally deal with the reality of losing a breast in one of three ways. First, some do nothing, preferring, for reasons of their own, simply to learn to adjust to their new body image. For some women, Susan Love points out, "refusing to create the illusion of a breast is part of their feminist beliefs." Love cites the example of an artist named Matushka, who

> created photographs of herself in a cutaway gown, showing not her remaining breast but the mastectomy scar. One photograph was on the cover of the *New York Times Magazine*. The effect is harsh and defiant, choosing to show the world what the disease of breast cancer does to a woman's body.[29]

Larger numbers of mastectomy patients opt for a prosthesis, an artificial, breast-shaped form they can wear inside a bra. And a number of others choose a third option for dealing with the loss of part or all of a breast—reconstructive surgery. This kind of plastic surgery can be done at the same time as the mastectomy or at any later time. Most doctors agree that the ideal time for reconstructive surgery is immediately following breast cancer surgery, while a woman is still on the operating table; this often eliminates the need for another surgical experience (though further surgeries are sometimes required).

Saline-filled breast implants like the one at left have been implanted in millions of women. The diagram below shows the basic steps of a TRAM-flap procedure for reconstructing the breast.

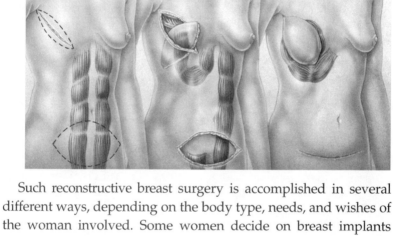

Such reconstructive breast surgery is accomplished in several different ways, depending on the body type, needs, and wishes of the woman involved. Some women decide on breast implants (filled with saline, silicone, or other fluids, such as soybean oil), which are usually placed behind the chest muscles (if these muscles have not been removed in a radical mastectomy). Another approach is to take muscle, skin, and fat from the woman's own belly area and use them as tissue flaps to form the new breast. This is called a TRAM-flap procedure. Muscles and fat can also be taken from a woman's buttocks or back for breast reconstruction. A woman who is considering reconstructive surgery should first discuss the option thoroughly with her doctor and plastic surgeon to choose the approach that is best for her. The bottom line, says the NIH, is that "the reconstructed breast will not have natural sensation, [yet] the surgery can give you a result that looks like a breast."[30]

The Role Played by Radiation Therapy

Like lumpectomy and mastectomy, radiation therapy (or treatment) is a local treatment that attacks the breast cancer within the breast and surrounding tissue. The kind of radiation generally used is high-energy X rays, which are aimed at the cancer cells in a narrow, carefully targeted beam. Because the radiation effectively kills cancer cells, surgeons almost always use it directly following a lumpectomy to make sure no malignant cells live on in the remaining breast tissue. (Doctors often call this step sterilizing the breast area.) The average schedule for such therapy is a session each day, five days a week for five or six weeks, each session lasting about five minutes. Radiation therapy is also frequently used after mastectomies. And in some cases, doctors employ such radiation *before* breast surgery to shrink the size of a tumor, so that it will be easier for the surgeon to remove later.

Years ago, when the technology for radiation therapy was new and less sophisticated, the X-ray beams were not as tightly focused. This produced more "scatter" of radiation into nearby skin and organs and caused various uncomfortable side effects, such as skin burns, trouble swallowing, and nausea. Today radiation scat-

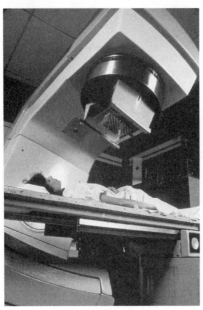

ter is very minimal, and such side effects are extremely rare. The National Cancer Institute says that a woman can expect to feel tired during her therapy; her skin in the treated area may feel dry, tender, itchy, or hard; or there may be some minor swelling around the nipple. These minor side effects are temporary and will disappear when the treatment is over.

This patient is about to undergo radiation therapy, a treatment often used following a lumpectomy.

A combination of two local treatments—surgery and radiation therapy—frequently helps women whose breast cancers are caught in the early stages. Thanks to education about breast cancer, early detection, and aggressive local treatment, a growing number of women who get the disease report success stories like that of a breast cancer survivor named Marcy: "We found it so early that my doctor was able to offer me [several] options. . . . We opted for lumpectomy with radiation. It turned out that the cancer was early stage, non-invasive, and lymph-node negative. I feel we really did make the right choice."[31]

Chapter 4

Systemic Treatments for Breast Cancer

USED TOGETHER IN various combinations, local treatment—surgery and radiation therapy—often prove effective against Stage 0, I, and II breast cancers (and some Stage III cancers). However, for many Stage II and most Stage III cancers, as well as all Stage IV cancers, doctors employ systemic treatments, those that affect the entire body rather than just the breast (or breasts). Unfortunately, systemic treatments, by definition, can harm some of the body's healthy cells along with the malignant ones. But if these therapies are properly and carefully applied, their unpleasant side effects can be minimized; the bottom line is that they are often highly effective in fighting cancer, especially in combination with local treatments. When doctors use systemic treatments as a follow-up to local treatments, the added treatments are called adjuvant therapy. (If, as happens in some cases, systemic treatments are used *before* surgery, to help shrink the size of a tumor, the systemic treatments are called neoadjuvant therapy.)

The most common and traditional systemic treatments are chemotherapy, the use of various drugs to kill the cancer cells; and hormonal therapy, which also uses drugs but in this case to keep the cancer cells from getting the hormones they need to grow. In addition, some women turn to what are usually referred to as complementary and/or alternative systemic treatments. (They are termed complementary when people use them *in combination with* conventional treatments; whereas the therapies are called alternative if people use them *instead of* conventional treatments.) Common complementary or alternative treatments include relaxation techniques, massage therapy, acupuncture, special diets, and vitamin and herbal regimens.

Choosing Chemotherapy

Chemotherapy is probably the best known systemic treatment for cancer, including breast cancer. The treatment is often discussed, both in the media and everyday life, in large part because it can

This bottle contains a mixture of potent chemotherapy drugs. Chemotherapy is the most widely used form of systemic cancer treatment.

have very noticeable side effects, such as hair loss, nausea, and fatigue. Not surprisingly, the potential bad side effects make most women with breast cancer reluctant to have chemotherapy, even when their doctors tell them that their situations warrant it. Yet many of these women end up going through with the therapy, mainly because they, and very often their spouses and other family members, worry what might happen if they do not. Typical is the story told by a breast cancer survivor named Gale:

> I kept saying, "I'm not interested in chemotherapy." And my doctor of thirty years was on my case every day. "We're going [to do it, he said,] and I'm going with you to hold your hand." And my husband was saying, "You know, we can't *not* do this." We were lying there in bed one night and . . . he said "I can stand anything unless I lose you." And I thought, Oh shit. I'm going to be in the middle of chemotherapy no matter what.[32]

In Gale's case, she and her doctor used chemotherapy as an adjuvant therapy. She had undergone a modified radical mastectomy. But four of her lymph nodes had tested positive for cancer, so it seemed prudent to follow up with the systemic drug treatment in hopes of destroying any stray cancer cells that might still linger in her body. This aim—to decrease the chances that a cancer will recur—is one of the three principal reasons for using chemotherapy. Studies have found that about 60 out of every 100 women with early-stage breast cancer (whose nodes tested negative) beat the disease with surgery and radiation. That leaves 40 percent of such women whose cancers can be expected to recur; and using chemotherapy as an adjuvant can reduce that figure to 15–20 percent. Deborah Axelrod puts it this way: "The surgery and radiation that treated the breast do nothing to fight cancer cells that may be lurking elsewhere in the body—and we don't yet have a tool with which to locate these hiding cells. Cancer drugs take up this fight where surgery and radiation cannot reach."[33] The other two main reasons for using chemotherapy are to shrink a large or inflamed tumor before surgery and to control (hopefully to slow the growth of) the cancer if it has metastasized to the lungs, liver, brain, and/or other parts of the body.

The Treatment and Its Side Effects

To be able to kill or control cancer cells, the drugs used in chemotherapy must necessarily be quite potent. In fact, for maximal effect, three powerful drugs are usually administered in combination. (The specific drugs and their exact combination vary from case to case, since some women may react better or worse to certain drugs. One of the most common combinations—called CMF—includes the drugs Cytoxan, methotrexate, and 5-fluorouracil.) The patients often receive the drugs intravenously, that is, by injection directly into a vein. However, sometimes chemotherapy drugs can be taken in pill form.

As for the duration and setting of the therapy, treatment can be as short as a few months or as long as two years. Doctors usually administer chemotherapy in cycles, during which the patient is treated for a period of time and then has a few weeks to recover before the

next treatment. Depending on the nature of the drugs used, the chemotherapy might be administered at home, in a doctor's office, in a clinic, in a hospital's outpatient department, or in a hospital. The frequency of chemotherapy treatments depends on the type and stage of breast cancer, the drugs administered, and how the body responds to them. The National Cancer Institute and other such organizations advise

Chemotherapy is available in hospitals, clinics, doctors' offices, and in patients' homes.

breast cancer patients to follow the schedule prescribed by their doctors and to check with their doctors before taking any other medications during treatment.

Because the drugs given in chemotherapy are designed to kill fast-growing cells (which cancer cells definitely are), they can also harm normal fast-growing cells. This is what produces the common unpleasant side effects of the treatment. Depending on the individual patient, the short-term side effects can include loss of appetite, nausea, vomiting, diarrhea, constipation, fatigue, bleeding, weight change, mouth sores, sore throat, and increased risk of infection. Some women also experience longer-term effects, among them damaged ovaries and early menopause (end of menstruation).

Today doctors are often able to lessen or control some of these side effects, although most women still experience at least a few of them. In general, individual reactions to chemotherapy vary widely from patient to patient. Some women who have undergone

Some patients experience unpleasant side effects during chemotherapy. These can include nausea, fatigue, and constipation, among others.

the treatment will readily identify with a breast cancer survivor named Julie, who sums up her experience with the terse phrase: "Chemo was hell."[34] Another survivor who had chemotherapy, Dana, a physical therapist, suffered from nausea so bad that she had to be hospitalized and receive replacement fluids intravenously. By contrast, other patients thankfully experience only minor side effects. "Chemo was not as devastating as I thought it would be," reports Sandy, a mother of five. "I was lucky I did not get very sick. After the treatment, for the next two or three days it was just like morning sickness [the nausea that often occurs in the initial stages of pregnancy], and the thought of food would just gag me."[35]

High-Dose Chemotherapy and Bone Marrow

So far, the kind of chemotherapy described is what might be termed the standard or traditional variety. In the late 1980s, a newer kind, often called high-dose chemotherapy, began moving from the experimental phase into accepted use by some doctors. As its name suggests, this treatment uses more potent doses of cancer-fighting drugs. It is designed, at least in theory, for that minority of women with breast cancer who do not respond well to the conventional local and systemic treatments, including surgery, radiation, and standard chemotherapy. Because their cancers tend to come back and often to metastasize, they are at a much higher risk of losing their battle with the disease.

The main problem with high-dose chemotherapy is that its side effects can actually be life-threatening. The drugs used are so strong that they damage the patient's bone marrow, where the body's lymphocytes are manufactured. Lymphocytes are white blood cells that play a major role in the body's immune response— its defensive reaction to germs and other harmful substances that invade it from the outside. Bone marrow also makes the red blood cells that carry oxygen throughout the body. By destroying bone marrow, therefore, high-dose chemotherapy damages both the patient's immune system and her or his ability to make new blood.

Clearly, high-dose chemotherapy would be a death sentence if doctors had no way to reverse its harmful effects on bone marrow.

Fortunately, two procedures have been developed to accomplish this task. One is called an autologous (meaning "from the patient's own body") bone marrow transplant. In Kathy LaTour's words, it

> involves removing about a quart of bone marrow from a woman before blasting her with [high-dose] chemotherapy. Then [after the drugs have done their work and left the body,] the bone marrow is reintroduced [via a needle], allowing it to rebuild the blood supply. It is, as one woman said, "taking a woman to the brink of death and then bringing her back with her own bone marrow."[36]

A doctor removes some of a patient's bone marrow. After the patient has undergone high-dose chemotherapy, the marrow will be replaced.

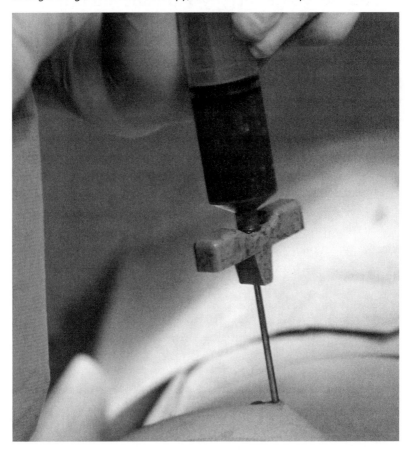

The other procedure, called an autologous stem cell transplant, is often used in conjunction with a bone marrow transplant as part of high-dose chemotherapy. A stem cell transplant involves the removal of a certain type of blood cell, called a stem cell, from a patient's blood. Stem cells are immature immune cells that eventually develop into various kinds of blood cells as the body needs them. Stem cells can make copies of themselves by dividing and forming more stem cells; or they can become fully mature red blood cells and white blood cells. After removing stem cells from a patient, technicians freeze the cells and store them while the patient is being treated with high-dose chemotherapy. After this treatment is over and the drugs are no longer in the woman's body, the technician returns the stem cells to the patient through a vein. The healthy stem cells can then begin to grow and produce the various kinds of blood cells the patient needs to survive.

It is imperative to emphasize that no strong clinical evidence has yet proven conclusively that high-dose chemotherapy is better than the standard variety. Nor do doctors know for sure exactly which patients will benefit most from the more potent drugs. Therefore, most physicians view high-dose chemotherapy as promising but still somewhat experimental; and clinical trials of the treatment continue. Another important point is that many insurance companies will not pay for this very expensive therapy, which they consider experimental; and those that do pay will cover only part of the costs. Thus, women and their doctors who are considering this approach must discuss and weigh a number of serious issues before proceeding with it.

Hormonal Therapy

Another systemic treatment for breast cancer—hormonal therapy—has side effects, too. But they are not nearly as severe or unpleasant as those associated with the various forms of chemotherapy. Hormonal therapy attempts to fight a cancerous tumor by starving it of the hormones it needs to grow. Lab tests indicate that some cancers depend in large degree on certain hormones, especially estrogen, to thrive. If a woman's lab test comes back saying that her cancer is "estrogen-positive," it means that her estrogen levels are giving her an increased risk of her cancer growing back even after she has had surgery and other treatments.

To prevent this from happening, doctors often administer hormone therapy as an adjuvant treatment after their patients have already undergone various local and/or systemic treatments. The hormonal therapy can be applied in one of two ways (or both). First, the doctor can give the patient an anti-estrogen drug, such as tamoxifen. (Other common ones include raloxifene, toremifene, and droloxifene, so that people often refer to these drugs as the "fenes.") Or the patient's ovaries, which produce estrogen, can be removed. In both cases, the levels of estrogen in a woman's body are significantly reduced, making it more difficult for any lingering cancer cells to grow into a new tumor.

The effectiveness of this strategy has been proven in clinical trials, which have shown that the treatment does significantly reduce the chance that some women's breast cancers will recur. And some studies have indicated that hormonal therapy cuts the chances of a woman getting cancer in her other breast in half. Moreover, by slowing the growth of some cancers, the therapy seems also to

This hospital pharmacist collects various drugs for use in a patient's hormone therapy. Such therapy is routinely administered as an adjuvant (additional) treatment.

help prolong the life of some women whose breast cancers have metastasized to other parts of their bodies.

As for the side effects of hormonal therapy, serious ones— including blood clots in the veins and formation of cancer in the lining of the uterus—are very rare. The most common side effects of the treatment are standard menopausal symptoms, such as hot flashes, nausea, vaginal discharge or dryness, irregular periods, and so on. According to Dr. Axelrod, these "are generally well tolerated," and only "about 5 percent of women [who undergo the therapy] will stop taking these drugs because of side effects."[37] A few women have even reported that the side effect of having fewer periods or none at all during their treatment made them feel better overall. "He [the doctor] put me on something [tamoxifen] that threw me into menopause," reports Madeline, a mother of two.

> I felt wonderful. I didn't have the mood swings like I get right before my period. Because that's when I would have my worst depression about all this [i.e., having cancer and cancer treatments]. . . . It took a couple of months for my periods to come back once I stopped taking it [the tamoxifen].[38]

It must be emphasized that hormonal therapy will not cure cancer all by itself; it works best in combination with other treatments.

Complementary and Alternative Treatments

The other treatments that accompany hormonal therapy most often include conventional, or "mainstream," ones such as surgery, radiation therapy, or chemotherapy. However, an increasing number of women are turning to complementary and alternative treatments (often called CAM, which stands for "complementary and alternative medicine"). The exact percentage of women who get breast cancer who try one or more CAM therapies during their conventional treatment (or instead of conventional treatment) is unknown. But it is revealing that a study of the use of CAM published in the July 2000 issue of the *Journal of Clinical Oncology* found that 83 percent of a group of 453 patients with cancer (all types) had used at least one CAM therapy as part of their cancer treatment.

The phrase "part of their cancer treatment" is the key to understanding the difference between complementary and alternative treatments and why most doctors are fairly accepting of one and wary of the other. As Susan Love explains, complementary treatments can be defined

> as supportive care used to decrease symptoms and to enhance the quality of a person's life, along with mainstream care. . . . Usually [complementary treatments] are medically safe. [They] include: meditation, counseling, diet, herbal supplements, yoga, certain teas, massage . . . [and] acupuncture. . . . None of these is considered a means of curing cancer, but only of working with the [conventional] medical treatment. Often surgery, chemotherapy, and the knowledge that you have cancer can bring on mild depression and anxiety, for example, and studies have shown that the herb St. John's wort can help moderate depression, while another herb, Kava Kava, can help with moderate anxiety.[39]

Similarly, according to the NIH, acupuncture has been found to be effective in the management of chemotherapy-associated nausea and vomiting and in controlling pain associated with surgery.

Among the various complementary treatments for breast cancer, yoga is popular. This woman holds herself in the so-called "accomplished" posture.

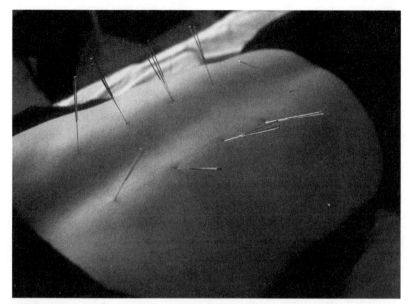

Acupuncture needles protrude from a cancer patient's back. Some women have reported positive results from using acupuncture as a complementary treatment.

By contrast, alternative treatments are used *instead* of conventional therapies. Alternative approaches sometimes include some of the same ones used in complementary medicine; they often also include a wide variety of others, among them megadoses of vitamins, all manner of special or unusual diets, using powerful magnets in hopes of healing cancerous tissues, ingesting shark cartilage and other unconventional substances, and many others.

The obvious question is whether such treatments can cure cancer, as some of their advocates claim. For the moment, though the answer is not necessarily a flat-out "no," there is no medical evidence yet to support this claim. So these and other unconventional treatments, when used alone, remain untested, unproven, and, in the opinion of most reputable doctors, risky at best. Most alternative treatments for cancer "have not been studied in any scientifically rigorous way," says Dr. Love, "and their risks are largely unknown. . . . I don't endorse their use."[40] Dr. Axelrod agrees, saying that she is leery about alternative therapies because "they are often recommended by destructive practitioners who

wrongly label chemotherapy as a 'poison.'"[41] Hirshaut and Pressman are especially emphatic about the risks of alternative treatments, which they call "a prescription for tragedy." They say that
when they see a large and already metastasized breast cancer in a
woman's first visit, it is almost always "when [she] comes to me
after being treated with unconventional treatments."[42]

A few doctors and other health care professionals may disagree
with these experts about the viability of alternative treatments.
Certainly, the use of CAM therapies in fighting breast cancer remains controversial. So perhaps the best, most prudent approach
for cancer patients considering complementary and alternative
therapies is to discuss such therapies with their doctors, just as
they would any important medical treatment.

Chapter 5

Readjusting to Life After Breast Cancer

A FTER A WOMAN undergoes treatment for breast cancer, her battle against the disease is far from over. She faces and must learn to deal with a wide range of physical, emotional, and lifestyle adjustments and issues, partly to ensure that her cancer is indeed cured and will not recur, and also to help her resume a healthy, productive life. These adjustments and issues include follow-up visits with her doctor and other members of her cancer care team; making sure that a support system (of relatives, friends, social workers, clergy, and/or others) is in place to help her both physically and emotionally; dealing with possible physical changes, such as premature onset of menopause, loss of sexual desire, and possible postcancer pregnancy; and general lifestyle changes that will help ensure a long and healthy life.

Follow-Up Care

It is imperative that women who have had local and/or systemic treatments for breast cancer follow up with regular exams and tests to make sure that the cancer has not come back, or that it has not appeared in the other breast. Most often the follow-up exams are scheduled once every six months for the first two years following the primary treatment; after that the woman goes for an exam once a year.

Regarding the exams themselves, doctors usually first look for lumps in the breast or the mastectomy scar. They also check the

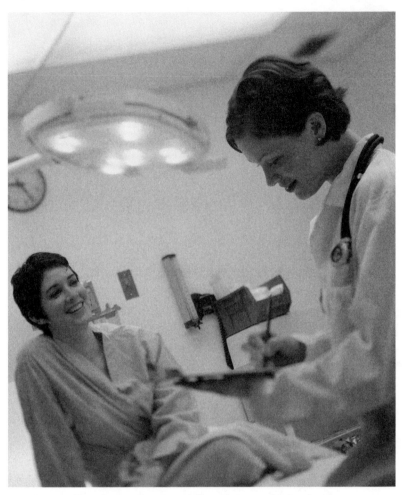

A patient and her doctor meet for a follow-up exam. Such exams are imperative for women who have undergone treatment for breast cancer.

neck and the area above the collarbone for lumps and feel under both of the patient's arms. A doctor typically questions the woman carefully, asking how she feels physically, and checks to see if she has had persistent and unusual pain in her legs or back, a persistent dry cough, or other symptoms suggesting that the cancer might have recurred. Most often, a doctor calls for a mammogram every six months for a year or two, and after this initial period, once a year. In addition to keeping an eye on the treated breast, the doctor watches the other breast to make sure no cancer has developed in it, since women with cancer in one breast have an increased risk of getting it in the other. Doctors recommend that such patients get an X ray of the untreated breast once a year. And depending on the case, some doctors do blood tests every three to six months and also liver blood tests, which can reveal the presence of metastatic disease in its earliest stage.

Fortunately, a majority of breast cancers do not recur and, to the relief of patients and doctors alike, the results of these careful follow-up exams more often than not prove negative. However, a significant minority of breast cancers *do* recur, even after the passage of several years; and that is why follow-up monitoring is essential once a year for an extended period, perhaps for life. "With breast cancer, unlike some other cancers," Love continues,

> we can't be sure that if it hasn't recurred within a few years, it won't. It's usually a slow-growing cancer, and there are people who have had recurrences 10 or even 20 years after the original diagnosis. . . . Time does, however, affect the *likelihood* of recurrence—the longer you go without a recurrence, the less likely you are to have one. So going 10 years without the cancer coming back should give you reason for optimism.[43]

Emotional Support from Family

While a woman's doctor and other medical professionals can see to the physical aspect of follow-up care, they can offer only so much emotional support. And every woman who faces breast cancer and the consequences of diagnosis and treatment does need emotional support, no matter how strong a person she was to begin with. As the NIH advises:

> [Having] breast cancer can change a woman's life and the lives of those close to her. These changes can be hard to handle. It is common for the woman and her family and friends to have many different and sometimes confusing emotions. . . . People living with cancer may worry about caring for their families, keeping their jobs, or continuing daily activities. Concerns about [medical] tests . . . and medical bills are also common.[44]

Thus, any woman facing a battle with breast cancer should try to make sure that she has a strong support network in place throughout the treatment and posttreatment phases of that battle. The most common and core people in such a network, of course, are family members, especially spouses or significant others, but also including children, parents, and siblings. On the negative side, some husbands lack the maturity and sensitivity to deal well with their wives' ordeals with breast cancer, offering little or no emotional support, and the eventual result can be separation or divorce. Fortunately, however, this appears to be the exception rather than the rule. "There seems to be a surprisingly low incidence of divorce among my patients," says Dr. Hirshaut.

A woman who has gone through breast cancer treatment poses with her family. Family members usually provide needed emotional support for such survivors.

Perhaps that is due to a reordering of priorities. . . . Perhaps having been through such a crisis together strengthens the relationship thereafter. Though everyone has heard or read about husbands and lovers who do not come through in a crisis, the overwhelming majority of them do.[45]

This was certainly the case with one breast cancer survivor, who, more than a year following her primary treatment, reported: "It's so strange, we used to have a lot of rocky times before, but it feels like this breast cancer thing has brought us closer together. I think when you have hard times, both people come to realize how much they rely on each other."[46]

Still, even when a husband or significant other sticks by the woman and supports her every step of the way, the experience is often a difficult and frustrating ordeal for that supporter. This shows how the disease takes its toll, to one degree or another, not only on the patient, but also on those closest to her. Take the example of Norm, whose wife, Lynne, survived a double modified radical mastectomy in 1982. "When your wife has cancer," he writes,

it's something you can't control. Here is something bad coming to attack your wife and you're the protector. How do you protect? And the answer is, you're helpless. There's not a blessed thing that you can do. You can't punch it in the nose. You can't sue it. You can't kill it. You've got to rely on the other people [doctors and other medical professionals] to take care of this thing for you.[47]

As it turned out, Norm *was* able to do something to help Lynne with her battle against cancer. Namely, he provided an ear to listen, a shoulder to cry on, a voice of encouragement and hope, a pair of hands to take care of household duties and errands, and other essential aspects of emotional and logistical support.

Children can also lend a breast cancer patient needed support. Both informing children about the cancer and seeking emotional support from them are sometimes difficult for the patient, who may feel that she has somehow burdened them by bringing the disease into the family. In most cases, though, such women find that their children take the news in stride and do everything they can to be supportive. Take the case of Susan, the mother of four who opted for a double mastectomy to be on the safe side:

> My first fears were that my children . . . would be burdened with this knowledge hanging over us for years to come. I felt sad and guilty for bringing this into our home, our lives. As a parent, I was used to being the caretaker, and now I felt I had somehow been removed from that role and was causing the family pain. I know [now that] this was irrational. . . . [Having gone through treatment with my husband and children by my side, I now have] faith, hope, and the unbelievably secure feeling I get just being surrounded by my family's love.[48]

Friends and Support Groups

Friends are another important element in a woman's support network. (Or they may be the primary element if the woman has no close family members within reach.) As in other kinds of crises that affect people's lives, women who have had breast cancer often discover who their real friends are. They may turn out to be true friends and supporters, as Lynne, Norm's wife, says hers were:

> I have a couple of best friends who I have had for years and they are the ones who never tried to fix things for me. They never tried to tell me what to do; they just listened. If I cried, they sat and held my hand, and that is all I wanted. That helped more than anything else, and I treasure those friendships.[49]

By contrast, some friends turn out to lack the closeness, empathy, and understanding needed for them to help a woman during and after breast cancer treatment. This was what a breast cancer survivor named Mickey experienced in the months after she underwent a mastectomy, chemotherapy, and hormonal therapy and became extremely depressed. "Right after surgery," she recalls, "when I started feeling like I was going to die and it [the cancer] was going to come back, my friends' response was, 'Don't worry, today they cure breast cancer. You will be fine.' They kept telling

One of these women is a breast cancer survivor, the other her friend. Close friends can be one of the most important links in a survivor's support network.

me how good I looked. I stopped talking to them."[50] Madeline, who had a mastectomy in 1988, also had some friends who patronized her or trivialized her ordeal by saying they understood what she was going through. In her view, "I think they need to say, 'I don't know what you're going through. But if you just want to talk and want somebody to listen to, I'm here for you.' But they shouldn't try to say they understand, because they can't."[51] On the other hand, another breast cancer survivor, Diane, urges others like her not to judge friends too harshly when they have trouble dealing with situations like hers: "People react differently [to such serious situations] . . . and that doesn't mean they don't care and that doesn't mean they don't love you and want to see you through it. Maybe they can't. And you need to give them a break, too."[52]

In addition to family and friends (or perhaps in place of them), various support groups and networks exist today to aid women during and after breast cancer treatment. Often a woman's doctor can recommend a local support group that offers individual counseling or can set up meetings between her and other women who have battled breast cancer. For some women, this approach is very helpful in their posttreatment rehabilitation. As a survivor named Joan puts it, "I just needed to talk to some women who had been through this and survived it."[53] A number of monthly or even weekly group meetings for breast cancer survivors exist in every state. Organizations such as Cancer Care (based in New York City) and the Women's Information Network Against Breast Cancer (in Covina, California) routinely provide information about support groups; and both the American Cancer Society and the NIH list such groups in booklets and on the Internet.

Group therapy sessions like this one allow breast cancer survivors to express their feelings and anxieties in a comfortable setting among understanding people.

Physical Adjustments

Besides medical checkups and the need for emotional support, a woman who has had breast cancer treatment almost always has to deal with certain physical changes that can alter her life in at least a few and often many ways. For example, one common bodily change that many women experience after having chemotherapy and/or hormonal therapy is the onset of menopausal symptoms, especially hot flashes (but also including vaginal dryness, trouble sleeping, and mood swings). These can be very uncomfortable at times. Depending on the age of the patient, these symptoms may be temporary and last perhaps one to three years. (In patients who are already in their late forties or fifties, the symptoms may end up being permanent, since these women would soon have entered menopause naturally anyway.)

A woman may or may not decide to seek remedies to reduce these symptoms. As Dr. Love points out, "Doing nothing is an acceptable choice. You don't have to treat or manage menopause unless it is interfering with your life."[54] For those patients who do want to reduce these symptoms, hormone replacement therapy (adding estrogen to the body) is an option for some (although it is still unclear if this increases the risk of the cancer recurring). Some doctors recommend eating soy or rubbing on special creams to help reduce hot flashes. Dr. Love suggests a behavioral approach to this problem, saying:

> Spicy foods, caffeine, stressful situations, and hot drinks are among the more common triggers [for hot flashes]. Once you've identified them, you can avoid them. Sleep in a cool room; carry a hand fan . . . walk, swim, dance, or bike-ride every day for thirty minutes or more.[55]

Another physical (as well as emotional) issue that affects some women after they have had breast cancer treatment is pregnancy. Most survivors of the disease, especially those already in their forties and fifties, choose not to get pregnant. However, a few do—mostly younger women who had few or no children before they got cancer. Dr. Hirshaut tells why this option is open to those women who want to pursue it:

Systemic treatments after surgery [especially chemotherapy and hormonal therapy] do interfere with fertility, but less so in younger women. I have a patient whom I first saw in her twenties. . . . After completing therapy she had five children. . . . Other former patients have had one or two children. It is not a common event, but for those who want a child, it is reassuring to know that it does happen. At one time it was thought that pregnancy might reactivate a previous case of breast cancer. There is no evidence that this is true.[56]

Lifestyle Changes

One good piece of advice doctors give women who face these and other posttreatment physical changes and issues is to adopt the healthiest lifestyle possible. This primarily means adopting a healthy diet and exercising regularly (quitting smoking, avoiding recreational drugs, and moderating alcohol consumption are also recommended). No evidence exists that eating right and exercising will ensure that one's breast cancer will not recur. However, there is no doubt that these behaviors will help cancer survivors feel better overall and make it easier for them to readjust their lives in the wake of their battle with the disease. "We do know," the NIH declares,

that eating right will help you regain your strength, rebuild tissue, and help you feel well. . . . Emphasize fruits and vegetables. Raw or cooked vegetables, fruits, and fruit juices provide the vitamins, minerals, and fiber you need. Emphasize breads and cereals, especially the whole grain varieties. . . . These foods are good sources of complex carbohydrates, vitamins and minerals, and fiber. Go easy on fat, salt, sugar, alcohol, and smoked or pickled foods. Choose low-fat milk products, and small portions . . . of lean meat and poultry without skin.[57]

Regular and vigorous exercise is also highly recommended for breast cancer survivors. (Such women should first ask their doctors how soon after treatment it is safe to start, since each woman's treatment and personal situation is different.) Dr. Love writes:

Any sport or exercise you did before your cancer you can do now—and you should, if you want to. If you've been a fairly

Doctors highly recommend regular and vigorous exercise for most breast cancer survivors. Good physical conditioning is beneficial for both body and mind.

sedentary [inactive] person, you might want to change that. . . . Not only will [exercise] make you feel better, but it will help you regain a sense of control over your body.[58]

Long walks, jogging, handball, tennis, dancing, swimming, and weight training (low weight, high repetition) are all effective ways to get back into and maintain good physical conditioning; and they can be mentally stimulating as well, as they often help to clear or refocus the mind.

It will obviously be easier for women who had healthy lifestyles before they faced breast cancer to resume them than it will be for those who had less healthy lifestyles before to adopt new healthy ones. But doctors and many survivors of the disease agree that in the long run the effort will be worth it. Adopting a healthy lifestyle reinforces and helps put a positive spin on the readjustment, reevaluation, and rethinking processes people usually undergo during and after cancer treatment. Almost inevitably, these processes make them see both themselves and life in general through new eyes. One such survivor, Wendie, sums it up eloquently:

> What cancer did was teach me . . . about myself. For one, it made me realize that I seriously had to start taking care of myself, which was very hard for someone like me, whose drug of choice has always been sugar. But the most important lesson I learned had nothing to do with food, and really had nothing to do with cancer! What I learned most was the importance of being okay with me, about loving and believing in myself. The cancer was a kind of wake-up call. It forced me to look at what was going on, what the lessons were in my life at the time.[59]

Chapter 6

The Future of Breast Cancer Treatment

THERE IS NO DOUBT that the traditional local and systemic treatments for breast cancer—surgery, radiation therapy, chemotherapy, and hormonal therapy—especially when used in combination, cure a large proportion of women who get the disease. But they don't help everyone. And those they do help usually must undergo months or years of anxiety, unpleasant physical side effects, and sometimes major changes in lifestyle and personal relationships. Not surprisingly, given these sober realities, medical science is constantly searching for new weapons in its anticancer arsenal, particularly those that show promise of stopping cancer in less invasive and life-altering ways. All over the world, hundreds of millions of dollars are spent each year by researchers searching for new and/or improved ways to fight cancer.

In light of the vast amounts of money and energy expended on such research, it seems justified to ask, Why hasn't a definitive treatment or cure for cancer, including breast cancer, already been found? Why is there no single, painless drug or other "magic bullet" to do the job? The answer to these questions is complex; but in a nutshell it has to do with the painstaking, methodical manner in which scientific research of this kind must proceed to produce the desired results. "The fact is," Deborah Axelrod points out,

> people fail to understand just how much room there is for failure in the course of scientific research. Of hundreds of other drugs and other therapies that are tested, only a tiny handful

make it to approval and widespread use. There are countless bumps in the road to drug development. One of the biggest is the basic difference between lab rats and human beings. . . . For example, a drug may be extremely effective in rats, but the human liver turns out to destroy the compound. Or maybe mice thrive on the drug, but most humans are allergic to it. . . . Many treatments fail for these sorts of practical problems—not because the underlying scientific principles are wrong, but because of forces outside of scientists' control. When you think about the infinite number of potential roadblocks to scientific research, it's a wonder so many effective treatments *do* eventually make it to the marketplace![60]

Despite these difficulties, some substantial progress has been made in cancer research in the past decade. And new, cutting-edge treatments, such as image-guided therapy and some forms

This medical researcher searches for new, more effective approaches to breast cancer treatment. Substantial progress has been made in recent years.

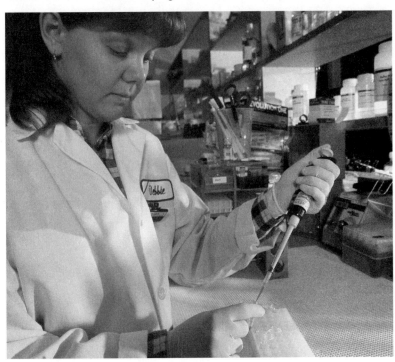

of biological therapy (or immunotherapy), are already being used on a limited basis. Meanwhile, other treatments, including anti-angiogenesis drugs (or angiogenesis inhibitors—substances that starve cancer tumors of the blood they need to grow) and cancer vaccines (another kind of biological approach), are still in the research or testing stages.

Image-Guided Therapy and Angiogenesis Inhibitors

One of the newest and most promising additions to the family of cancer treatments, image-guided therapy uses the best available imaging techniques to aid a surgeon in removing or neutralizing a cancerous tumor without the need for conventional surgery. MRI, originally used only in *diagnosing* cancer, is the imaging technique most often used to help *treat* breast cancer. Image-guided therapy allows surgeons "to safely guide their operating instruments directly to the site of disease through the smallest of incisions," reports the U.S. Public Health Service's Office on Women's Health.

> Image guidance allows the surgeon to see beneath the patient's skin without open surgery and allows diagnosis and treatment to be performed less invasively. . . . Recently, new data has emerged demonstrating that small cancers can be removed by using imaging to guide needles into the tumor to administer direct tumor treatment by heating (e.g., laser surgery, [or] focused ultrasound) or freezing. . . . When MRI is coupled with focused ultrasound, the treatment is completely noninvasive, and there is no need for skin incision.[61]

This technique was used in clinical trials in the 1990s to treat benign breast tumors; and some doctors are presently employing it against malignant tumors in experimental procedures.

While image-guided therapy aims to neutralize cancerous tumors, angiogenesis inhibitors attempt to keep such tumors from growing larger or even to shrink them. "Angiogenesis"is the scientific term for the formation of new blood cells in the body. When a tumor first appears as a small cluster of cells in a person's body, it has no direct access to the person's bloodstream, so it usually grows only very slowly. But at some crucial point, the tumor undergoes a transition (which is not yet well understood) and begins drawing on the person's blood supply. Then the tumor grows more rapidly. Angiogenesis inhibitors are drugs that are designed to stop tumors from getting the blood they need. According to the National Cancer Institute, "In animal studies, angiogenesis inhibitors have successfully stopped the formation of new blood vessels, causing the cancer to shrink and die."[62] Such drugs are now being tested on humans, as well.

Biological Therapy

Biological therapy also has as its goal the destruction of cancerous tumors but tries to attain that goal without using surgery or drugs. Instead, the various biological approaches under development induce or help the body's own immune system, either directly or indirectly, to fight cancer. Basically, the immune system consists of a complex network of organs, cells, and proteins (complex organic molecules) that work together to fight off antigens (germs or other foreign substances that invade the body). Among the many kinds of immune system cells and proteins are the B lymphocytes (or B cells), which make antibodies (tiny, aggressive proteins that recognize and then neutralize antigens by attaching themselves to them); T lymphocytes (or T cells), which attack infected and cancerous cells, as well as antigens; and cytokines, proteins that either help coordinate the attack on antigens or actually join in that attack. The main goal of biological therapy is to stimulate the production of these cells and proteins and get them to kill cancer cells.

In one promising form of biological therapy, researchers or technicians manufacture antibodies, cytokines, and other immune-system substances in the laboratory. They then inject them into cancer patients. The researchers attempt to "tailor" these substances to do specific tasks. Among these tasks are helping to slow or halt the growth of cancerous cells, making cancer cells more recognizable (and therefore more vulnerable) to the immune system, blocking or reversing the process that changes a normal cell into a cancerous one, and preventing cancer cells from spreading

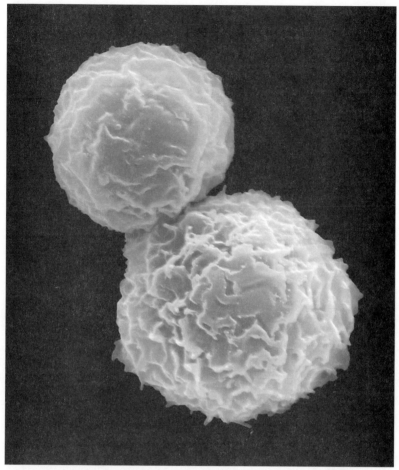

This image, taken with an electron microscope, shows a human helper T cell
(top) and a B cell, both specialized lymphocytes that aid in the body's
immune response.

through the body. One group of such substances—interferons—
have proved quite effective in clinical trials. The National Cancer
Institute describes interferons as

> types of cytokines that occur naturally in the body [and are eas-
> ily made in labs]. Researchers have found that interferons can
> improve the way a cancer patient's immune system acts against
> cancer cells. In addition, interferons may act directly on cancer
> cells by slowing their growth or promoting their development

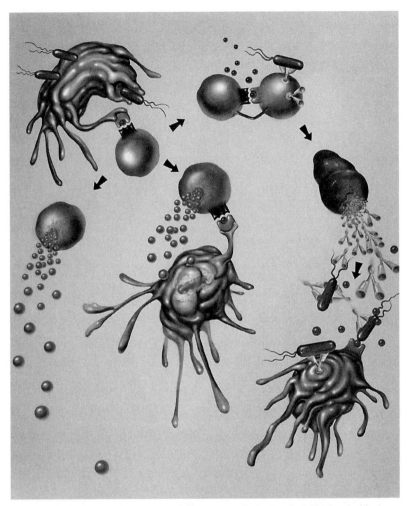

A medical illustration depicts interferons (the small round objects) stimulating white blood cells (the large irregular cells) to attack foreign or abnormal cells.

into cells with more normal behavior. Researchers believe that some interferons may also stimulate [various lymphocytes], boosting the immune system's anti-cancer function.[63]

The U.S. Food and Drug Administration (FDA) has approved one kind of interferon for use against some forms of cancer. Scientists are presently exploring ways to use other types of interferons, as well as similar substances, to fight breast cancer.

Vaccines to Fight Cancer?

A more familiar kind of biological approach to fighting disease—vaccines—has been in use for well over a century. However, only in the late 1970s did certain crucial scientific breakthroughs allow researchers to begin searching for ways to make anticancer vaccines. A vaccine is a substance made from germs, parts of germs, or other tiny pieces of a specific disease; they provide protection against that disease by stimulating the body's immune response against it without passing on the disease itself. For example, the polio vaccines pioneered in the 1950s and 1960s use polio viruses that have been killed or weakened to immunize people against the disease. (The viruses in the vaccines are not strong enough to make people contract polio, but they do cause the body's immune system to recognize these germs and attack them vigorously in any future infections.)

A considerable amount of research is presently under way at labs around the world to create and perfect effective cancer vaccines. Such vaccines might not *prevent* cancer from growing in the first place, as vaccines for polio prevent the onset of that disease in

A scientist prepares a dose of an experimental anticancer vaccine. Labs around the world are presently attempting to develop such vaccines.

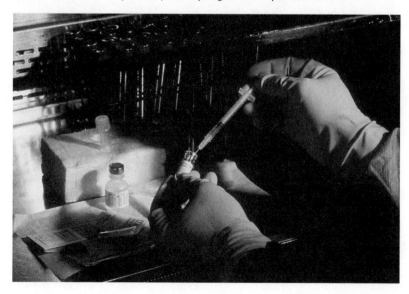

a healthy person. After all, cancer cells are not germs or foreign invaders, but cells that grow within a person's own body. However, by stimulating a large, specifically targeted immune response, effective cancer vaccines could conceivably keep existing cancerous tumors from growing large enough to require traditional, often invasive, and sometimes dangerous treatments.

Not surprisingly, the main difficulty in developing a cancer vaccine that fights a specific kind of cancer is getting the body's defensive cells both to recognize and to attack the abnormal cells of that type of tumor. In the early years of the twentieth century, scientists learned that antibodies, the special proteins manufactured by white blood cells, are skilled at recognizing differences between cells and other substances in the body. Antibodies can detect tiny distinctions among antigens and normal body cells by recognizing specific molecules coating their outer surfaces, in a sense molecular "fingerprints."

Later researchers found that, like invading antigens and normal body cells, cancer cells have their own distinctive fingerprints. (Scientists came to call these cancer-cell fingerprints antigens, after the foreign-invader type of antigen.) But in the case of most kinds of cancer, these distinctive antigens were apparently invisible to the antibodies; this explained why a cancerous tumor could grow larger and larger without provoking a full-scale attack by the immune system. If scientists could devise some way to make the antigens coating the cancer cells visible to the immune system, they might be able to target a certain kind of cancer with a vaccine based on antibodies that recognized that specific cancer. The problem was where to get such specially programmed antibodies. The sad reality was that researchers lacked the technical means to produce large numbers of a specific kind of antibody, both for study and use in a vaccine, before 1975.

Antibody Cancer Vaccines

Medical science finally began to overcome that limitation in 1975 thanks to two scientists working at the University of Cambridge, in England. Cesar Milstein and Georges J. F. Kohler found a way to fuse (bring together as one) normal antibody-making cells with cancerous cells taken from a mouse. The result was cells that reproduced and grew into a mass, just as cancer cells do, but that also produced antibodies. Moreover, the cells in any single mass were clones of one another, and therefore all identical; and similarly, all of the antibodies they produced were of the same kind. For this reason, Milstein and Kohler, who received the Nobel prize for their achievement, called them monoclonal ("one clone") antibodies.

Since that time, researchers have been working on several different approaches to using antibodies to create cancer vaccines. In one, the antibodies target the antigens of specific cancer tumors. Injected into the cancerous area of a patient, such an "antigen vaccine" would hopefully stimulate the body to produce large numbers of T cells, which would zero in on and destroy the cancer cells bearing the targeted antigen. Another antibody vaccine under development attempts to rig the antibodies to carry toxic (poisonous) substances, such as plant toxins and various radioactive compounds, directly to tumors.

A lab technician prepares slides containing monoclonal antibodies for use by researchers. The hope is that such antibodies will target specific kinds of tumors.

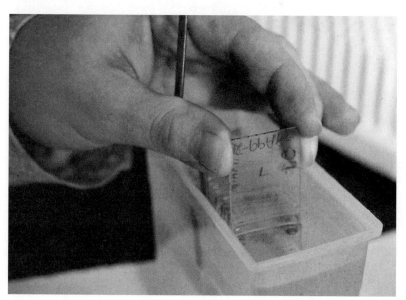

Still another approach that shows promise involves engineering antibodies to attack the stroma, the tissue that connects one cancerous tumor cell to another. The stroma makes up as much as 60 percent of any cancerous mass; and without it, a tumor cannot grow past microscopic size, in which case it remains harmless to the body. In the late 1990s, researchers at the Memorial Sloan-Kettering Cancer Center in New York City identified certain antigens that coat the stroma; and this may well lead to a vaccine that directs the immune system to attack the stroma.

A Prognosis for Breast Cancer's Future

Other innovative cancer vaccines presently under development use approaches that focus on other agents besides antibodies. One of these agents is a less-familiar soldier in the body's army of microscopic defenders—the dendritic cell. Dendritic cells, which regularly patrol the body, carry around tiny bits and pieces of harmful germs and use these pieces as markers to show other immune cells, such as the killer T cells, which invaders to attack. Scientists make dendritic cell vaccines by extracting some of the patient's dendritic cells and then reproducing large numbers of dendritic cells in the laboratory. The researchers expose these dendritic cells to antigens that have been extracted from the patient's cancer cells. They then inject this mixture of dendritic cells and antigens into the patient; and the dendritic cells begin to program the T cells with information identifying the specific cancer antigen involved.

It is important to emphasize that these and the dozens of other cancer vaccines now in various stages of development are far from perfected. There still is no magic bullet for breast cancer, or any other kind of cancer. And the end of the quest for a cure for cancer is still not clearly in sight. Indeed, although researchers have enjoyed some considerable success with new and emerging therapies, drugs, and vaccines, it is still too early to predict if medical science will develop a method or methods that will completely eradicate cancer. If that momentous goal is indeed attainable, it will not be achieved in the near future. However, most experts are confident that new advances in research will, in the foreseeable future, at least bring cancer, including breast cancer, under control

These people are crossing the finish line in the June 2000 "Race for the Cure," in which participants helped raise money for breast cancer research.

and make deaths from the disease very rare. Reflecting this positive view, Dr. Axelrod offers the following prognosis for breast cancer's future:

> I believe that with the advent of new therapies, new diagnostic tools, and new ways of determining women at greatest risk of getting breast cancer, we will soon be able to manage even advanced breast cancer as a chronic illness—not unlike diabetes, for example. . . . I see a time in the very near future in which even those women with relatively advanced breast cancer will live long, productive lives with this disease in check. . . . The fights won't necessarily be easy, and they certainly aren't fun, but women will increasingly be the winners. And there will be countless elderly grandmothers telling of their battles with breast cancer.[64]

Notes

Introduction: Winning the Battle Against Fear

1. Quoted in Deborah Axelrod and Rosie O'Donnell, *Bosom Buddies: Lessons and Laughter on Breast Health and Cancer.* New York: Warner Books, 1999, p. 1.
2. Quoted in Axelrod and O'Donnell, *Bosom Buddies,* p. 139.
3. Quoted in Axelrod and O'Donnell, *Bosom Buddies,* p. 1.
4. Yashar Hirshaut and Peter I. Pressman, *Breast Cancer: The Complete Guide.* New York: Bantam, 2000, p. 296.

Chapter 1: Breast Cancer Types, Survival Rates, and Risk Factors

5. Hirshaut and Pressman, *Breast Cancer,* p. 9.
6. Quoted in BreastCancer.org, "How Breast Cancer Happens," April 2001. www.breastcancer.org/cmn_und_idx.html, p. 2.
7. National Institutes of Health (NIH), "What You Need to Know About Breast Cancer," December 2000. www.cancernet.gov/wyntk_pubs_breast.htm, p. 3.
8. Susan Love, *Dr. Susan Love's Breast Book.* Cambridge, MA: Perseus Publishing, 2000, pp. 220–22.
9. Love, *Dr. Susan Love's Breast Book,* p. 221.
10. NIH, "What You Need to Know," p. 3.
11. Axelrod and O'Donnell, *Bosom Buddies,* pp. 13–14.

Chapter 2: Screening for and Diagnosing Breast Cancer

12. American Cancer Society (ACS) Breast Cancer Research Center, "Detection and Symptoms," September 2000. www.3.cancer.org/cancerinfo/load_cont.asp?st=ds&ct=5&language=english , p. 4.
13. ACS, "Detection and Symptoms," p. 4.
14. Love, *Dr. Susan Love's Breast Book,* p. 317. Dr. Love bases her opinion in large part on a study that began in 1997 of some 267,000 women in Shanghai, China. The women were divided into two groups, one whose members received instruction in

doing self-exams and who performed the exams regularly, and one whose members received no instruction and did not perform regular self-exams. The preliminary results were that the breast cancers that developed in the women in the first group were not detected any earlier than those of the women in the second group. And death rates from breast cancer were the same for both groups. For more detail, see D. B. Thomas et al., "Randomized Trial of Breast Self-Examination in Shanghai: Methodology and Preliminary Results," *Journal of the National Cancer Institute,* vol. 89, 1997, pp. 355–65.

15. Hirshaut and Pressman, *Breast Cancer,* pp. 52–53.
16. Quoted in Axelrod and O'Donnell, *Bosom Buddies,* p. 51.
17. Quoted in Kathy LaTour, *The Breast Cancer Companion.* New York: William Morrow, 1993, p. 36.
18. Quoted in Faina Shtern et al., eds., *Image-Guided Diagnosis and Treatment of Breast Cancer.* Washington, DC: U.S. Public Health Service's Office on Women's Health, 1998, p. 16.
19. Hirshaut and Pressman, *Breast Cancer,* pp. 67–68.
20. ACS, "Detection and Symptoms," p. 6.

Chapter 3: Local Treatments for Breast Cancer

21. Quoted in BreastCancer.org, "Treatment," May 2001. www.breastcancer.org/tre_surg_adv.html, p. 1.
22. Axelrod and O'Donnell, *Bosom Buddies,* p. 142.
23. Axelrod and O'Donnell, *Bosom Buddies,* p. 150.
24. National Institutes of Health, "Understanding Breast Cancer Treatment." http://rex.nci.nih.gov/PATIENTS/aboutbc/ubc_treatment.html. "Surgery," p. 2.
25. From a previously unpublished interview with breast cancer survivor Susan Sopkin, June 5, 2001.
26. Quoted in LaTour, *Breast Cancer Companion,* pp. 107–108.
27. LaTour, *Breast Cancer Companion,* p. 108.
28. Quoted in LaTour, *Breast Cancer Companion,* p. 108.
29. Love, *Dr. Susan Love's Breast Book,* p. 445.
30. NIH, "Understanding Breast Cancer Treatment," "Surgery," p. 8.
31. Quoted in BreastCancer.org, "Treatment," p. 2.

Chapter 4: Systemic Treatments for Breast Cancer

32. Quoted in LaTour, *Breast Cancer Companion,* p. 134.
33. Axelrod and O'Donnell, *Bosom Buddies,* p. 162.
34. Quoted in LaTour, *Breast Cancer Companion,* p. 135.
35. Quoted in LaTour, *Breast Cancer Companion,* p. 147.
36. LaTour, *Breast Cancer Companion,* p. 188.
37. Axelrod and O'Donnell, *Bosom Buddies,* p. 170.
38. Quoted in LaTour, *Breast Cancer Companion,* pp. 172–73.
39. Love, *Dr. Susan Love's Breast Book,* pp. 497–98.
40. Love, *Dr. Susan Love's Breast Book,* p. 509.
41. Axelrod and O'Donnell, *Bosom Buddies,* p. 190.
42. Hirshaut and Pressman, *Breast Cancer,* p. 93.

Chapter 5: Readjusting to Life After Breast Cancer

43. Love, *Dr. Susan Love's Breast Book,* pp. 519–20.
44. NIH, "What You Need to Know," p. 15.
45. Hirshaut and Pressman, *Breast Cancer,* p. 283.
46. Quoted in Hirshaut and Pressman, *Breast Cancer,* p. 283.
47. Quoted in LaTour, *Breast Cancer Companion,* p. 478.
48. Interview with Susan Sopkin.
49. Quoted in LaTour, *Breast Cancer Companion,* p. 265.
50. Quoted in LaTour, *Breast Cancer Companion,* p. 266.
51. Quoted in LaTour, *Breast Cancer Companion,* pp. 266–67.
52. Quoted in LaTour, *Breast Cancer Companion,* p. 265.
53 Quoted in LaTour, *Breast Cancer Companion,* p. 267.
54. Love, *Dr. Susan Love's Breast Book,* p. 542.
55. Love, *Dr. Susan Love's Breast Book,* p. 551.
56. Hirshaut and Pressman, *Breast Cancer,* p. 283.
57. National Institutes of Health, "Eating Hints for Cancer Patients Before, During, and After Treatment," publication #98-2079, July 1997, p. 2.
58. Love, *Dr. Susan Love's Breast Book,* p. 521.
59. Quoted in Axelrod and O'Donnell, *Bosom Buddies,* p. 220.

Chapter 6: The Future of Breast Cancer Treatment

60. Axelrod and O'Donnell, *Bosom Buddies,* pp. 253–54.
61. Quoted in Shtern et al., *Image-Guided Diagnosis,* p. 23.
62. National Cancer Institute, "Angiogenesis Inhibitors in the

Treatment of Cancer," July 1998. http://nci.nih.gov/fact/pdfdraft/7_therap/fs7_42.pdf, p. 1.

63. National Cancer Institute, "Biological Therapies: Using the Immune System to Treat Cancer," January 2001. http://cis.nci.nih.gov/fact/pdfdraft/7_therap/fs7_2.pdf, p. 4.

64. Axelrod and O'Donnell, *Bosom Buddies*, p. 238.

adjuvant therapy: Any cancer treatment used after or in addition to primary treatment.

alternative treatments: In relation to cancer, unconventional methods or treatments used instead of, rather than in addition to, conventional treatments.

ambulatory procedure: Surgery or other treatment in a hospital that allows the patient to go home on the same day as the treatment.

antibodies: Proteins manufactured by the body's white blood cells to help defend against invading disease germs.

antigen: A harmful substance, usually part or all of a disease germ that invades the body. The term is also used to describe chemical "fingerprints" on the surfaces of germs and various body cells.

autologous: Taken from a person's own body.

autologous bone marrow transplant: A procedure (part of high-dose chemotherapy) in which some of a patient's bone marrow is removed before chemotherapy and then reintroduced into her or his system after the drugs are no longer present.

autologous stem cell transplant: A procedure (part of high-dose chemotherapy) in which some of a patient's stem cells (immature blood cells that can readily multiply) are removed before chemotherapy and then reintroduced into her or his system after the drugs are no longer present.

biopsy: Removal of tissue from the body, using a needle or surgery, for the purpose of diagnostic examination.

breast ducts: The small tubes connecting the lobes, lobules, and milk bulbs in the breast.

breast lobes and lobules: The major sections of the breast, containing the milk-producing bulbs.

chemotherapy: The use of drugs to kill cancer cells. An extreme form—high-dose chemotherapy—uses extremely potent drugs that also destroy the patient's bone marrow tissue.

complementary treatments: In relation to cancer, unconventional methods or treatments used in addition to conventional treatments.

core needle biopsy: A biopsy that uses a thick needle and removes up to half an inch of material from a suspected tumor.

cytokines: Proteins that, as part of the body's immune response, either help coordinate the attack on antigens or actually join in that attack.

drains: In relation to recovery from breast cancer surgery, small tubes that carry away excess fluid that can build up in the breast area following surgery.

ductal carcinoma in situ (DCIS): A kind of breast cancer confined to the breast ducts.

estrogen: Any of a group of female hormones produced mainly in the ovaries. The body manufactures estrogen to produce secondary female sexual characteristics and also to prepare the uterus for pregnancy. Estrogen is also an ingredient of birth control pills and various hormonal therapies.

excisional biopsy: A surgical biopsy in which all of the suspected tumor is removed.

false negative: In diagnosis, a test result that appears normal even though a disease or other abnormality is actually present.

false positive: In diagnosis, a test result that detects a disease or other abnormality when no such problem is actually present.

fine needle aspiration biopsy (FNAB): A biopsy that uses a thin needle to remove material from a suspected tumor.

hormonal therapy: In relation to cancer, the use of drugs or other means to starve cancer cells of the estrogen they need to grow.

hot flashes: Sudden, temporary sensations of heat experienced by some women during menopause.

immune response: The body's defensive reaction to harmful substances that invade it from the outside.

incisional biopsy: A surgical biopsy in which only part of the suspected tumor is removed.

interferons: A group of cytokines that occurs naturally in the body and that was also the first cytokines manufactured in a lab for use in biological therapy for cancer.

intravenous: Administered directly into the bloodstream, usually through a vein.

invasive (or infiltrating) ductal carcinoma (IDC): A kind of breast cancer in which the tumor spreads from a duct to nearby breast tissue.

invasive (or infiltrating) lobular carcinoma (ILC): A kind of breast cancer in which the tumor spreads from a lobe or lobule to nearby breast tissue.

lobular carcinoma in situ (LCIS): A kind of breast cancer confined to the lobes of the breast.

local treatment: Relating to breast cancer, a type of treatment that deals primarily with the breast that contains the cancer.

lumpectomy (or wide excision): The surgical removal of a breast tumor and a small amount of neighboring tissue, leaving most of the breast intact.

lymph nodes: Small oval-shaped organs located to the sides of the breasts under the arms, in the chest, and in various other parts of the body. The vessels connecting the lymph nodes carry a clear fluid called lymph, which removes bacteria from the blood and also circulates protective white blood cells.

lymphedema: A postoperative condition that sometimes affects women who have had mastectomies in which their underarm lymph nodes have been removed. The lymph does not circulate properly and causes the arm and hand to swell.

lymphocyte: A white blood cell that manufactures or aids in the manufacture of the body's defensive forces during an immune response.

mammogram: An X-ray picture of the breast.

mastectomy: Usually the surgical removal of part or all of the breast, along with some of the underarm lymph nodes. In a radical mastectomy, the most extensive kind, all of said lymph nodes and also the chest muscles beneath the breast are removed.

menopause: The period during which the body naturally ceases menstruating (having periods each month); menopause most often occurs between the ages of 45 and 55, but symptoms can appear earlier, especially among women who have undergone systemic breast cancer treatments.

metastasis (or metastatic disease): The spread of cancer cells (or other disease-producing organisms) from the primary site of the disease to other parts of the body, most often by way of the lymph vessels and nodes.

monoclonal antibodies: Antibodies produced by special cells created by fusing antibody-producing cells with cancer cells. The special cells reproduce, each new copy a clone of and therefore identical to the others; and the antibodies these cells create are all of a single type.

MRI (magnetic resonance imaging): A technique that uses a powerful magnetic field to create images of various parts of the body.

Paget's disease: Breast cancer of the nipple and/or its surrounding area.

papillary carcinoma: A kind of breast cancer characterized by cancerous cells that look like little fingers.

PET scan (positron-emission tomography): A technique that creates images of various parts of the body by detecting a mildly radioactive fluid injected into the body.

prosthesis: As it relates to women who have had mastectomies to treat breast cancer, an artificial form that a woman can wear inside her bra to create the illusion of a real breast.

reconstructive surgery: As it relates to breast cancer patients, the creation, through surgical means, of a new breast to replace one removed during a mastectomy.

sonogram: An image created of the breast or another part of the body using sound waves.

stroma: The tissue that connects one cancer cell to another.

systemic treatment: Relating to breast cancer, a type of treatment that affects the rest of the body in addition to the breast.

tamoxifen: The most common anti-estrogen drug used in hormonal therapy to fight breast cancer cells.

T cells: Short for cytotoxic T lymphocytes: These are special lymphocytes that can attack various foreign antigens, as well as virus-infected cells. They are often called "killer" T cells.

toxin: A poison.

TRAM-flap procedure: A kind of reconstructive breast surgery in which muscles, skin, and fat from the patient's belly area are used to create a new breast.

tubular breast cancer: A kind of breast cancer characterized by cancerous cells that look like little tubes.

vaccine: A substance that provides protection against a specific disease by triggering the body's natural immune system without passing on the disease itself.

American Cancer Society
1599 Clifton Rd. NE
Atlanta, GA 30329
(800) 227-2345
Internet: www.cancer.org

Provides information about all types of cancer and helps support research into cancer treatments and preventions.

Cancer Care
1180 Avenue of the Americas
New York, NY 10036
(212) 221-3300
e-mail: info@cancercareinc.org
Internet: www.cancercareinc.org

Offers free assistance to those who have cancer, including information, counseling, referrals, and financial assistance.

The Chemotherapy Foundation
183 Madison Ave., Suite 403
New York, NY 10016
(212) 213-9292

Promotes the use of drugs to cure, control, or prevent cancer; also educates doctors, nurses, cancer patients, and the public about chemotherapy.

Foundation for the Advancement of Cancer Therapy
P.O. Box 1242, Old Chelsea Station
New York, NY 10113
(212) 741-2790

Educates cancer patients, members of their families, and also the public about alternative treatments for cancer.

Helping Children Cope Program of Cancer Care
(800) 813-HOPE
Internet: www.cancercare.org

Provides support groups and telephone counseling for children who have a parent who has cancer.

Mothers Supporting Daughters with Breast Cancer
Internet: www.mothersdaughters.org

A national nonprofit group offering support services for mothers who have daughters fighting breast cancer.

National Alliance of Breast Cancer Organizations (NABCO)
9 East 37th St., 10th Floor
New York, NY 10016
(888) 806-2226
e-mail: NABCOinfo@aol.com
Internet: www.nabco.org

Provides a fulsome list of books, pamphlets, and so on dealing with breast cancer.

National Breast Cancer Coalition
1707 L St. NW, Suite 1060
Washington, DC 20036
(202) 296-7477
Internet: www.natlbcc.org

A coalition of more than five hundred local groups dedicated to changing public policy so as to encourage progress in the fight against breast cancer.

The Susan G. Komen Breast Cancer Foundation
5005 LBJ Freeway, Suite 370
Dallas, TX 75244
(972) 855-1600
e-mail: education@komen.org
Internet: www.breastcancerinfo.com, also www.komen.org

Dedicated to eliminating breast cancer through research, education, and proper treatment; offers educational information about breast cancer and breast care.

Women's Information Network Against Breast Cancer
19325 East Navilla Place
Covina, CA 91723
(626) 332-2255
Internet: www.winabc.org

This nonprofit organization offers resources, peer support, and referral information via telephone counseling, mail, and community outreach.

Y-Me National Breast Cancer Organization
c/o Susan Nathanson
212 West Van Buren
Chicago, IL 60607-3908
e-mail: help@y-me.org
Internet: www.y-me.org

Provides educational materials about breast cancer in both English and Spanish.

For Further Reading

Books

Claire Blake et al., *The Paper Chain.* Oxford, England: Health Press, 1998. Geared to children aged three to eight, this book deals with the reactions of two young boys whose mother gets breast cancer.

Faith H. Brynie, *101 Questions About Your Immune System You Felt Defenseless to Answer . . . Until Now.* Brookfield, CT: Twenty-first Century Books, 2000. A well-organized, informative introduction to the body's immune system. Cancer researchers focus most of their attention on trying to make the immune system recognize and fight breast cancer and other forms of cancer.

Christine Clifford, *Our Family Has Cancer Too!* Duluth: Pfeifer-Hamilton Publications, 1997. A boy struggles to understand and deal with his mother's cancer in this well-written book aimed at grade school and junior high readers.

Leatrice Lifshitz, *Her Soul Beneath the Bone: Women's Poetry on Breast Cancer.* Champaign: University of Illinois Press, 1988. A collection of thoughtful and sometimes highly moving poems, including selections by F. M. Bancroft, Alice J. Davis, Lorene Erickson, Zona Gale, Patricia James, Elizabeth Lincoln, and several others. Though the poems are not aimed directly at young people, teenagers, especially young women, will find them easy to read, straightforward, and emotionally compelling.

Laura Numeroff and Wendy S. Harpham, *Kids Talk—Kids Speak Out About Breast Cancer.* Dallas: Samsung Telecommunications America and Sprint PCS, 1999. A collection of short stories told by children whose mothers have breast cancer.

Ruth Pennbaker, *Both Sides Now.* New York: Henry Holt, 2000. A teenage girl's life turns upsidedown before she finally finds that she has the inner reserves of strength needed to cope with her mother's breast cancer. Well written and moving.

Carole G. Vogel, *Breast Cancer: Questions and Answers for Young Women*. Breckenridge, CO: Twenty-first Century Books, 2001. Loaded with important information about breast cancer, this book's question-and-answer format and straightforward writing style make it highly accessible to young women.

Internet Sources

MGH Hotline Online, "Teen Reaches Out to Children of Breast Cancer Patients at the Massachusetts General Hospital," July 2, 1999. www.mgh.harvard.edu/DEPTS/pubaffairs/issues/070299teenkits.htm.

James Swinburne (aged ten), "Mum's Breast Cancer," 1996. www.nbcc.org.au/pages/women/children.htm.

Works Consulted

Books

Roberta Altman, *Waking Up/Fighting Back: The Politics of Breast Cancer*. Boston: Little, Brown, 1996. Examines in well-documented detail the medical and social attitudes toward breast cancer, as well as controversial aspects of mammograms and other kinds of diagnosis, surgery, and the general state of modern breast cancer research.

Deborah Axelrod and Rosie O'Donnell, *Bosom Buddies: Lessons and Laughter on Breast Health and Cancer*. New York: Warner Books, 1999. This book, written in an engaging style by Axelrod and peppered with humorous passages by O'Donnell, is one of the best and most up-to-date general sources on the entire spectrum of breast cancer issues for the layperson. Highly recommended.

Yashar Hirshaut and Peter I. Pressman, *Breast Cancer: The Complete Guide*. New York: Bantam, 2000. Two leading medical authorities cover all major and most minor aspects of the subject in an easy-to-read format and style. Highly recommended.

Kathy LaTour, *The Breast Cancer Companion*. New York: William Morrow, 1993. One of the best general books about breast cancer, partly because it contains numerous short, often moving first-person quotes by women who have lived through the various stages of the disease.

Susan Love, *Dr. Susan Love's Breast Book*. Cambridge, MA: Perseus Publishing, 2000. Without doubt, the largest, most comprehensive book about breast cancer on the market. Love is a fount of information and her documentation is fulsome and impressive. The reader should be warned, however, that she goes into great detail on every topic and that her writing style is sometimes on the scholarly side. The layperson will find Axelrod and O'Donnell's book and Hirshaut and Pressman's volume (see above) more accessible.

Giselle J. Moore-Higgs et al., *Women and Cancer*. Sudbury, MA: Jones and Bartlett, 2000. This excellent general reference book, written for nurses and nursing students, contains a long, informative chapter on breast cancer.

Stanley A. Plotkin et al., eds., *Vaccines*. St. Louis: W. B. Saunders, 1999. A well-written, reliable general reference book on the subject.

Faina Shtern et al., eds., *Image-Guided Diagnosis and Treatment of Breast Cancer*. Washington, DC: U.S. Public Health Service's Office on Women's Health, 1998. This short but informative volume contains descriptions and evaluations of the various existing and also emerging imaging techniques (from mammography to MRIs and beyond) used in diagnosing and also treating breast cancer. Also contains numerous helpful color pictures.

George F. Vande Woude and George Klein, eds., *Advances in Cancer Research*. San Diego: Academic Press, 1999. A compilation of highly informative, up-to-date, mostly scholarly articles on the present state of cancer research, including that related to breast cancer.

Periodicals, Booklets, and Reports

Anna Aldovini and Richard A. Young, "The New Vaccines," *Technology Review*, January 1992.

Lawrence K. Altman, "Drug Shown to Shrink Tumors in Type of Breast Cancer by Targeting Gene Defect," *New York Times*, May 18, 1998.

R. W. Blamey et al., "Screening for Breast Cancer," *British Medical Journal*, September 16, 2000.

Rowan T. Chlebowski, "Primary Care: Reducing the Risk of Breast Cancer," *New England Journal of Medicine*, July 20, 2000.

Kristen L. Finn, "Breast Cancer: Alternatives to Mastectomy," *USA Today*, May 15, 1995.

Elizabeth M. Jaffe, "Progress Toward Cancer Vaccines," *Hospital Practice*, December 15, 2000.

Gina Kolata, "Mammogram Talks Prove Indefinite," *New York Times*, January 24, 1997.

D. W. Kufe, "Smallpox, Polio and Now a Cancer Vaccine?" *Nature Medicine*, March 6, 2000.

K. McPherson et al., "Breast Cancer: Epidemiology, Risk Factors, and Genetics," *British Medical Journal*, September 9, 2000.

National Institutes of Health, "Eating Hints for Cancer Patients Before, During, and After Treatment," publication #98-2079, July 1997.

Lloyd J. Old, "Immunotherapy for Cancer," *Scientific American*, September 1996.

David Perlman, "2 New Breast Cancer Drugs Ok'd by FDA's Advisory Panel," *San Francisco Chronicle*, September 3, 1998.

M. A. Richardson et al., "Complementary/Alternative Medicine Use in a Comprehensive Cancer Center and the Implications for Oncology," *Journal of Clinical Oncology*, July 2000.

J. R. C. Sainsbury et al., "Breast Cancer," *British Medical Journal*, September 23, 2000.

D. B. Thomas et al., "Randomized Trial of Breast Self-Examination in Shanghai: Methodology and Preliminary Results," *Journal of the National Cancer Institute*, vol. 89, 1997.

J. Travis, "Fused Cells Hold Promise of Cancer Vaccines," *Science News*, March 4, 2000.

David B. Weiner and Ronald C. Kennedy, "Genetic Vaccines," *Scientific American*, July 1999.

Internet Sources
Author's Note: The sources listed below are all recognized as highly reputable; the information they provide is supplied by doctors and other medical professionals and can therefore be trusted. Unfortunately, though, the Internet's vast depository of information also contains numerous less reliable sources that advocate untested theories about and supposed cures for cancer, as well as misinformation and half-truths about the disease. Those seeking extensive information on the subject, or any medical subject, should first go to the following site, provided by the National Cancer Institute. It explains in a simple, step-by-step manner how to evaluate the worth and reputability of a site offering medical information. "10 Things to Know About Evaluating Medical Resources on the Web," July 1999. http://cancertrials.nci.nih.gov/beyond/evaluating.html.

American Cancer Society Breast Cancer Research Center, "Detection and Symptoms," September 2000. www.3.cancer.org/cancerinfo/load_cont.asp?st=ds&ct=5&language=english.

Deborah Axelrod, "What You Should Know About Breast Cancer." www.breastdoc.com.

Kevin Bonsor, "How Cancer Vaccines Will Work." www.howstuffworks.com/cancer-vaccine.htm.

Breast Cancer Answers, "Personal Stories." www.canceranswers.org/stories/index.htm.

BreastCancer.org, "How Breast Cancer Happens," April 2001. www.breastcancer.org/cmn_und_idx.html.

———, "Myths About Breast Cancer," May 2001. www.breastcancer.org/cmn_myt_idx.html.

———, "Treatment," May 2001. www.breastcancer.org/tre_surg_adv.html.

———, "Understanding Clinical Trials: It's Not About Being a Guinea Pig," May 2001. www.breastcancer.org/res_clin_idx.html.

CancerNet, "Screening for Breast Cancer," May 2001. www.cancernet.nic.nih.gov.

Alfred E. Chang, "Cancer Vaccines: A Primer About an Emerging Therapy," January 2000. www.cancernews.com/vaccines.

A. G. Dalgleish, "Cancer Vaccines and Gene Therapy: Current Clinical Trials," St. George's Hospital Medical School. www.tustison.com/dal.htm.

HHS News, "Breast Cancer Detection Rates by Race and Ethnicity Show Importance of Screening for All Age Groups," October 2000. www.hhs.gov/mews/press/2000pres/20001012a.html.

National Alliance of Breast Cancer Organizations, "Abnormal Mammograms," June 1999. www.nabco.org/resources/index.html.

———, "Facts About Breast Cancer in the U.S.A.," February 2001. www.nabco.org/resources/index.html.

———, "Questions and Answers: Young Women and Breast Cancer," June 1999. www.nabco.org/resources/index.html.

National Cancer Institute, "Angiogenesis Inhibitors in the Treatment of Cancer," July 1998. http://nci.nih.gov/fact/pdfdraft/7_therap/fs7_42.pdf.

———, "Biological Therapies: Using the Immune System to Treat Cancer," January 2001. http://cis.nci.nih.gov/fact/pdfdraft/7_therap/fs7_2.pdf.

———, "Breast Cancer Risk Assessment Tool." http://bcra.nci.nih.gov/brc/learnmore.htm.

———, "Financial Assistance for Cancer Care," September 2000. http://cis.nci.nih.gov/fact/8_3htm.

———, "Improving Imaging Methods for Breast Cancer Detection and Diagnosis," March 1997. http://cis.nci.nih.gov/fact/5_14.htm.

———, "Questions and Answers About Adjuvant Therapy for Breast Cancer," April 2000. http://cis.nci.nih.gov/fact/pdfdraft/7_therap/fs7_20.pdf.

———, "Questions and Answers About Complementary and Alternative Medicine in Cancer Treatment," December 2000. http://cis.nci.nih.gov/fact/pdfdraft/9_unconv/fs9_14.pdf.

———, "Questions and Answers About Screening Mammograms," November 2000. http://cis.nci.nih.gov/fact/5_28.htm.

———, "Sexuality: Supportive Care—Patients," May 2001. www.cancernet.nci.nih.gov.

National Institutes of Health, "Understanding Breast Cancer Treatment." http://rex.nci.nih.gov/PATIENTS/aboutbc/ubc_treatment.html. Has numerous links to separate articles, including "Chemotherapy," "Hormonal Therapy," "Surgery," "Reconstructive Surgery," and so on.

———, "What You Need to Know About Breast Cancer," December 2000. www.cancernet.gov/wyntk_pubs_breast.htm.

David Olle, "Cancer Vaccines," January 23, 2001. www.suite101.com/article.cfm/9718/57009.

Kathleen I. Pritchard, "Breast Cancer Immunotherapy: A New Hope?" 2nd International Breast Cancer Research Group Conference, June 2000. www.medscape.com/medscape/CNO/2000/

BCIRG/public/conference.cfm?-conference_id=64.

Reuters Medical News, "Animal Model of Hereditary Breast Cancer Created," 2001. www.medscape.com.

————, "Cancer Vaccine Shows Promise Against Colorectal Cancer," 2001. www.medscape.com.

————, "MRI May Be Best Diagnostic Tool for Women at High Risk of Breast Cancer," 2001. www.medscape.com.

————, "Tests Under Development to Allow Individualized Breast Cancer Risk Projection," 2001. www.medscape.com.

————, "Ultrasound-Guided Mammotome Breast Biopsy Safe and Reliable," 2001. www.medscape.com.

WebMDHealth, "About Male Breast Cancer," 1999. http://my.webmd.com/content/dmk/dmk_article_5963021.

Index

factors, 20
on exercise, 72–73
on feminism and breast
cancer, 46
on handling physical
changes from cancer
treatments, 71
on multiple causes, 19
on recurrence, 65
on self-examination, 27–28
lumpectomy, 39, 40–42
lymph nodes, 16, 17
lymphocytes, 55, 78

magnetic resonance imaging.
See MRI
malignancy, 17
mammogram, 26, 28–31
digital, 82
"markers," 32
mastectomies, 45–47
double, 44
modified radical, 42–43
partial, 42
radical, 39, 43
segmental, 39
simple, 42
total, 42
Matushka, 46
M. D. Anderson Cancer
Center, 34
Memorial Sloan-Kettering
Cancer Center, 84
menopause, 54, 71
metastasis, 15, 39
methotrexate, 53
Milstein, Cesar, 82–83

MRI, 33–34

National Cancer Institute, 31,
46, 48, 53–54, 79–80
National Coalition for Cancer
Survivorship, 45
National Institutes of Health
(NIH)
on acupuncture, 60
on diet for cancer survivors,
72
on metastasis, 17–18
on need for emotional
support, 65
publications of, 70
on reconstructed breasts, 47
NIH. *See* National Institutes of
Health
nipple, 16, 17
Nobel Prize, 83

ovaries, 54, 58

Paget's disease, 17
papillary carcinoma, 17
PET (positron-emission
tomography) scan, 34
pregnancy, 71–72
Pressman, Peter I., 11, 13–14,
28, 34–35, 62
prosthesis, 46

race, 20
radiation
as causing cancer, 21–22,
39–40
as therapy, 48–49

Picture Credits

Cover Photo: © Samuel Ashfield/FPG International LLC
© AFP/CORBIS, 85
American Cancer Society, 26
Linda Bartlett/National Cancer Institute, 36, 39, 83
© Barts Medical Library/Phototake, 43
© Bettman/CORBIS, 9, 28
© Bohemian Nomad Picturemakers/CORBIS, 61
Stephen S. T. Bradley/CORBIS, 21
Bill Branson/National Cancer Institute, 10, 30, 51
© Thomas Brummett/CORBIS, 64
© Steve Chen/CORBIS, 73
© Allen Dex/Publiphoto/Photo Researchers, 25
© Ronnen Eshel/CORBIS, 60
Donald Gates/National Cancer Institute, 41
© Julie Habel/CORBIS, 66
© Jack Hollingsworth/CORBIS, 69
© Impact Visuals/Phototake, 45, 53
Chris Jouan, 13, 16
John Keith/National Cancer Institute, 81
© Dennis Kunkel/Phototake, 79
Dr. Lance Liotta Laboratory, 18
National Cancer Institute, 15, 29, 48
© Richard T. Nowitz/CORBIS, 70
Photo Researchers, Inc., 35
© Reuters NewMedia Inc./CORBIS, 47
© Bob Rowan/Progressive Image/CORBIS, 58
Suza Scalora/PhotoDisc, 54
Mitchell D. Schnall, M.D., Ph.D. University of Pennsylvania, 33
© SIRI MILLS/Phototake, 80
© Leif Skoogfors/CORBIS, 56
© Kevin A. Somerville/Phototake, 47
© Robert Trubia/CORBIS, 23
© Bill Varie/CORBIS, 76

About the Author

In addition to his numerous acclaimed volumes on ancient civilizations, historian Don Nardo has published several studies of modern scientific and medical discoveries and phenomena. Among these are *The Extinction of the Dinosaurs, Eating Disorders, Cloning, Vaccines,* and a biography of Charles Darwin. Mr. Nardo lives with his wife, Christine, in Massachusetts.